ALPHA'S ENSLAVED BRIDE:
A TERRAMATES NOVEL

LISA LACE

CONTENTS

CHAPTER 1

QUINN

Predicting the future sounds exciting until you wake up one day knowing what's going to happen. Take it from me - it's not exciting at all. Fucking visions. I wish I never had a single one.

When the egg hit me in the head, it broke immediately. I felt the sticky yolk run down into my black hair. I knew it was official.

I was an outcast.

As I crouched in the street with egg dripping down the side of my face, I was determined not to cry. My breathing was ragged, and my chest heaving with effort, but I would not show weakness in front of these bastards. The men who humiliated me would never get the satisfaction of knowing that they had broken me, no matter how torn up I felt inside.

I couldn't kneel forever. I stood up slowly, wiping the raw egg from my face. I wondered where they got the credits to afford real eggs.

Maybe the farmer down the road was a member of their cult, too. They called themselves a church, but everyone knew what it really was, even me and my dad.

We hadn't been in this town long. My hometown was the little community of Core Rock, a charming mining settlement. There were exactly two hundred sixteen inhabitants - actually, two hundred fifteen now that Abigail had gone away to school.

I lived a happy childhood there. My family consisted of my father, who was also my best friend. I did well in school, and my life was perfectly normal until I was fourteen.

That was when the visions started.

At first, I thought I was lucid dreaming until they began to happen during the day. I managed to hide everything until I had one at school. They thought I was having a seizure. My father had me tested for epilepsy, but the tests came back negative.

I almost wish I had been suffering from some unfortunate disease, but that wasn't my fate. As it turned out, I was a psychic and could see into the future.

It's a rare ability on Earth, but I have learned that aliens on other planets exhibit these powers all the time. Unfortunately for me, I didn't live on these other planets. My harassment by my fellow humans began almost immediately. Earthers, in general, have not caught up to other interstellar cultures in regards to peace, harmony, understanding, and tolerance.

At first, people started teasing me at school. It escalated quickly to bullying. I got beat up a couple times. "Why didn't you see that punch was coming, you freak!"

I couldn't control when I had visions, or what I saw.

My father didn't know what to do. He went to the police, but they couldn't do anything. He tried to protect me by dropping me off and picking me up at school. Someone always found a way to get to me when there wasn't anyone else looking.

Things became complicated when I foresaw someone's death. A kid at school was planning to commit suicide, and I knew it was going to happen. I tried to do something about it. My plans didn't work, and he died. Despite my best intentions, I drew suspicion upon myself. An investigator suspected me, and they nearly charged me with murder.

That's when my dad and I decided to move. I started hiding my ability. I ignored the next death I saw in my visions. If I knew someone was going to be hurt, I watched movies until the early morning hours so I could fall asleep.

If I was exhausted, sometimes I could avoid the nightmares.

My father was distraught and tried to help me. We went to see everyone we could — doctors, healers, a shaman. Someone who claimed to be able to exorcise demons. Nothing worked. In fact, my visions became more intense and more accurate. As I got older, I wanted to change the future. I wanted to prevent bad things from occurring, especially the deaths that I saw. Every time I started, I remembered what happened in Core Rock and didn't do anything.

Now they had found me again in our new town. I didn't know how the Sons of the Heavenly Father kept tracking us down. News agencies have linked them to murders all over Earth, but they only target a specific minority - people who are different, like me. If the eggs were the best weapons they had, they'd find they would need to do a hell of a lot more than that to scare me away.

I pivoted on my right foot, turning in a circle. On a whim, I raised my hands like claws.

"Stand back," one man yelled.

I heard a few of them muttering. They all held up crossed index fingers. I heard the word 'witch' multiple times. If they wanted me to be a witch, I supposed I could play the part. I knew it was a bad idea, but something in me was so angry and so sick and tired of running away that I couldn't seem to stop myself.

I pushed my hands away from myself, palms facing away, and I screamed. As loud as I could, like a banshee.

I saw the crazy men's faces turn white. They stumbled backward as if they'd been knocked down by the simple act of me raising my hands. For a moment, as they ran away, I got a false sense of power. I felt like a witch. I could make the bad guys cower.

But I was just an ordinary girl.

I began walking as fast as I could back to the apartment I shared with my father. I knew young women should be out on their own to learn independence. But I wasn't a typical girl. My dad needed me and helped me with my visions. If I had an unexpected seizure, he was there to protect me. Since I couldn't work, he supported us. I avoided people and typically ventured out at dusk.

Today had been such a beautiful day I couldn't stay inside any longer. I went for a walk. The men found me, pelting me with eggs and calling me rude names. I was lucky they didn't beat me up, but I was still anxious.

"They *knew* that you have a gift? They said so?" my father said. His brown eyes looked calm, but I didn't need powers to know he was terrified. His hands were shaking.

"They called me a witch, Dad. That says it all, I think."

"We've worked so hard to escape from the Sons of the Heavenly Father. It's discouraging to know they've found us again. We may need to run."

"They're not going to stop. We know what they do to witches. We've seen it on the news." My father shuddered, probably remembering the images of charred remains in his mind. The Sons of the Heavenly Father were on a quest to burn anyone they accused of being a witch - all in the name of their savior, of course. History was repeating itself. They thought the ends justified the means. They believed their salvation was worth murdering innocent lives. I wondered what their god thought about that.

I felt the need to confess.

"I might have made it worse, Dad. I'm sorry."

He sighed, closing his eyes wearily. "What did you do, Quinn?"

"It's possible I lifted my hands and screamed like an animal," I said, apologetically, demonstrating my pose.

My father shook his head. "Oh, Quinn. If they didn't think you were a witch before, they'll know you are now."

"I know," I said sadly. "I know. We have to go right away, Dad. We can't bring anything." We hadn't accumulated much. It had only been six months since we moved here. I had a feeling it wouldn't be the last time.

I felt a sense of longing for home that was so strong it almost overpowered me for a moment. I didn't have a place to call home anymore. I could no longer go back to Core Rock. Not even for a visit. I didn't think my life wasn't in danger here, but I still felt afraid.

Dad said we had to wait until nightfall to leave. "We'll be less conspicuous if we leave in the evening," he said. "In the meantime, you should pack and rest. We may be up all night, Quinn."

9

"Okay, Dad," I said, going quietly to my room.

This vision was clearer than any I had ever experienced before. Every detail was vivid, even the smell of the snow. Who knew snow even had a smell? Not me. We didn't get snow where I lived on Earth.

The air was crystal clear. My breath came out of my mouth like smoke. The cold stung my cheeks as I walked through the forest.

Sometimes the visions I had felt like watching a movie. I was never in the movie. I was always an observer.

Until now.

This time, I was one of the people in the story, and I was playing myself.

I was walking alone through the snow. I needed to get away from something. The storm drove into my face at one moment and into my back the next. Huge trees whipped back and forth in the wind. Since I had arrived on this planet, I had never seen the trees moving like this. I had seen severe winds before, but they barely moved the branches. Now enormous tree trunks were swaying back and forth and groaning. I started to feel afraid. What if one of them fell on me?

I tripped suddenly. Not only my boot, but my entire foot was caught under a root. I hadn't seen it under the deep snow. I was stuck. I struggled, trying to free it, but it wouldn't come out. What was I going to do now?

Without warning, I heard a crack and a big tree began to fall on top of me. I stared up in fear, holding up my arms uselessly in a futile attempt to protect me. I was saved when the trunk caught on another tree and stopped falling.

A voice yelled my name behind me. I had never heard it before, but it seemed familiar.

"Quinn!" I turned to look and saw a man yelling and beckoning to me. I knew he was good looking, but somehow his face remained out of focus. I couldn't see his features. "Come on!"

He came up to me and pulled on my arm.

"My foot's stuck. Get out of here," I said, pushing at him, feeling afraid and desperate. "We don't both have to die."

The man smiled at me, then glanced up at the fallen trunk. It was beginning to creak. The tree could start falling again at any time.

He took my hands in his and leaned towards me. His eyes were full of emotion. "We do both have to die. I love you. And I can't live without you."

"What?" I said.

"I love you," he said again. This time, he leaned in and kissed me.

When the tree hit us, it was over so quickly I barely felt a thing.

When I emerged from a vision, I saw two worlds at the same time. The forest scene began to dissolve. Simultaneously, the ceiling of my bedroom came into focus. My father sat at the foot of my bed.

"Was it a bad one, Quinn?" he said. His voice sounded worried. "You were tossing and turning a fair bit."

I sat up, trying to remember everything. The images of the forest began to slip away like a dream.

"I don't know."

"Tell me, Quinn. You know you remember better when you tell someone."

My body felt shocked by grief, but I wasn't sure why.

"Quinn?" My dad put his hand on top of mine. "Are you all right?"

"No," I said. "I just watched myself get crushed with a man I'm going to love."

"What?"

"I was in my vision," I said, turning my eyes to him at last.

"You were *in* the vision?"

"Yes, it was a vision about me."

"Has that ever happened before?" he asked.

"Not that I can remember," I said.

"Hm." He looked troubled for a moment. Then he stood up. "Time to go, I think."

"Yes," I said, trying to calm down and come back to reality. Sometimes after a vision, it was difficult for me to return to real life. I stood up and grabbed my emergency bag. "I'm ready."

I followed my father down to the main floor and into an attached garage. We got in the car and drove away. We weren't coming back.

CHAPTER 2

QUINN

Blackness surrounded us and kept us safe as we drove down the dark highway. We sped away from a place that had never felt like home. I drove while my father slept. He would take the second shift. I wondered where we would go. It didn't matter as long as we remained hidden.

When I noticed the car behind me, I initially dismissed it. As it crept closer yet never passed us, I felt terror creeping up on me. Had the Sons of the Heavenly Father followed us? I hadn't imagined that possibility. What if someone had been watching our house? Would they do that?

I had the impression that the Sons of the Heavenly Father, although murderous, were a bunch of dumb, unsophisticated hicks with poor organization. In my mind, only a bunch of rednecks and bullies would go around burning people in this day and age.

If they had followed us, it meant there were some people in their organization that had brains and were able to use them. They were more than typical bullies. They were intelligent, coordinated bullies.

I hoped the car was an elderly grandma that didn't want to pass us at night, but my idealistic dream didn't ring true. I knew it was them. Sometimes I have hunches that seem like something more, and they're usually right. I've learned to listen to my gut. Dad calls it my 'sick sense'. He has an odd sense of humor.

If it was them, I needed to decide where to go immediately. I shouldn't go to an isolated location. I should drive us to a mall or some other place with lots of people. That should keep me safe. They were known to get their victims alone to hurt or kill them. None of the reported attacks had any witnesses — at least, none left alive to tell their tale.

I sped up and frowned at my rear-view mirror when the car behind us kept pace. Damn. My father snoozed on, and I debated whether to wake him or not. I decided to wait a little longer. When I turned off the road, I would know if the car was following us. I didn't need Dad's advice for that. I also didn't want to say my fear out loud because that would make my terror real.

I passed a sign that said the next town was ten miles away, and I drove on. My hands gripped the wheel so tightly my fingers started to ache. When we drove through the town, I realized it was too small a place to turn or stop because the sleepy village was already closed for the night. It was only eight o'clock, but nothing was open.

I needed to continue until I hit a big city, and find a place where people were awake and businesses were open. The next half hour passed slowly. Our pursuers remained behind us. I still nursed a faint hope. Any number of people could be going to the city. It was the only one in the area, and all the communities shopped there for items they couldn't get at home. It wasn't unreasonable to think someone else was going there and not pursuing me.

The problem was the dreadful feeling in my guts. It told me that something was very wrong.

When we arrived at the city, Dad finally woke up. "Quinn?" he said, yawning and stretching his arms. "Where are we?"

"We're in the city already. I'm afraid that someone might be following us."

He turned around. "It's the black car," I said, praying that I was wrong.

"What do you think we should do?"

"I thought that we should go somewhere to hide in a crowd."

"Quinn, if that's the Sons of the Heavenly Father, why do you think they're following us?"

"To kill me," I whispered.

"We need to go to the police immediately. There's no need to risk your life."

I glanced over at him and then back at the road. "You're right."

He found the nearest police station and sent the coordinates to the car. I put it on autopilot, and it proceeded to get us there in a few minutes. There was nowhere to park on the front side of the building, where civilians were allowed to enter. Maybe there was a staff entrance in the rear next to the parking lot.

"I'll drop you off. You run into the building," Dad said. "They're not that close to us. You'll have time to get in. Don't stop until you're safely inside."

"Okay," I said, pulling over. As soon as the car stopped, I jumped out and moved towards the door of the police station. It had no windows — probably to keep them from being broken all the time in a seedy neighborhood like this one. Out of the corner of my eye, I saw the black car pulling up behind us. The window opened, and I raced for the door. I reached the steps and scrambled up as quickly as I could.

As I reached for the handle of the door, I felt something sting my neck. I put my hand up to feel a dart embedded in my skin. Pain shot through my neck, and it started swelling immediately. I looked around and saw shadowy figures running toward me. I tried to move. My legs weren't responding to my brain. Then my legs collapsed, and I felt myself falling. Before I hit the ground, I was out.

AIRIK

I sat up in bed. Sweat rolled down my face. My eyes were open, but I didn't see the world around me. I was having a Precog.

As soon as I realized what was happening, my training kicked in automatically.

"Precog," I said. My computer beeped and began recording my speech, as well as my brainwaves and other vital signs. Saying the keyword also alerted the ground crew back at headquarters. The team worked continuously to record and interpret our visions.

I began to describe what I was seeing. It took Precogs a lot of training before we could speak while having a vision. After ten years of working for the Precog Division and recording over a thousand visions, I had the hang of it.

"Someone's following me," I said. "I'm in a vehicle."

"Which planet are you on?" came the familiar voice of Miroll, my regular Recorder.

"I don't know. The car is driving itself. Does that help?"

"Did you say a car?"

"Yes, it's a car," I said, feeling mildly annoyed.

"Continue to monitor your surroundings for signs of the location," Miroll's calm voice instructed me through the communications unit I wore behind my ear. "What else do you see?"

"It's night. I'm scared."

"Are you male or female?"

I glanced down at my hands and clothes. I had breasts. There were some things about being a Precog I would never think were normal.

"Female," I said.

"Why are they following you?" she asked gently.

"I don't know. I think someone wants to hurt me."

"Hurt you how?"

"I'm not sure. This sounds ridiculous, but I think they want to burn me."

Miroll continued with her quiet questions. She asked me what I could see and what was happening. She wanted to know the colors, sights, smells, and sounds. Recorders were trained to get as many pertinent details out of Precogs as possible before the vision ended.

"She's important, Miroll."

"Please estimate on a scale of one to ten." We were taught to give the importance of the person in a vision a number.

"Eleven," I said immediately. I could sense Miroll's surprise. "Wait. There's a road sign coming up," I said. As it got closer, I inspected it. The writing was in an unfamiliar language to me. Fortunately, the words were not unfamiliar to this woman's body, and I could understand them in the vision. "Or-land-oh? Ten miles," I said, reading it aloud.

"Spelling please," Miroll's gentle voice requested.

"O-r-l-a-n-d-o. It's sweltering here, Miroll."

"Yes, you've said that..." There was a pause as she counted under her breath. "Five times, sir."

They were going to a police station. She was traveling with a man, and she was afraid of the people in the car behind her.

I felt the woman jump out of the car and sprint for the doors of the police station. Something pinched her neck, and I felt her pass out.

"She's unconscious," I said.

"How did that happen?" Miroll asked, sounding surprised.

In real life, I heard a noise. I crashed back into reality as my girlfriend, Sornalee, walked into my room.

"Hey babe, why are you still awake?" Her voice trailed off when I glared at her. "Were you working?"

She had the grace to look like she was sorry. Being sorry wouldn't bring back the scene in my mind. I hadn't found out why she fell unconscious. The woman might die if we didn't do anything, but now I had no way to learn how she would be knocked out.

"When I receive a Precog, a light activates on my door. That means that you can't come in, Sornalee."

"I know, Airik, I know. I forgot to look."

"I was having a Precog about an important person in a dangerous situation. You interrupted before I could get enough information to save them."

"Oh no." She put a perfectly manicured hand up to her lips. Sornalee was the picture of dismay, but I sensed she was annoyed.

I completed my call with Miroll, but there wasn't much more to say. My vision was gone. Sornalee got into bed with me, but neither one of us could sleep.

When I asked Sornalee to move in, it seemed like it would be perfect. We had been dating for over a year and a half. I thought I knew her. She understood the difficulties and challenges of my job. She was tall, blonde and loved sex. What could go wrong?

As it turned out, everything could go wrong. After a few weeks of living together I realized I had made a terrible mistake with Sornalee. She was terrific in small doses, but I couldn't stand to be around her all the time. Before, I could go home when she started annoying me, or I could hang up the phone, and she vanished in an instant. I could ask her to leave if I needed to work.

Not anymore. Sornalee was a constant presence in my life. She rarely left because she didn't have a job. Her father was independently wealthy. She had a trust fund in her name that provided her with more than enough to survive.

I don't know what she did all day, but she was always home when I needed a break, except for girl's night out. I needed to end this and tell her to move out. I couldn't believe I had been ready to ask her to marry me. That would have been a nightmare - being saddled with her for the rest of my life.

"Sornalee, you know I care about you."

She frowned. "I don't like how this conversation is starting. You're not breaking up with me, are you?"

"I'm afraid we're not working out," I said, shaking my head.

"Is this because I walked in on one of your stupid visions?" she said. "What a waste of time. I can't believe I went out with you. Now I only have six months to find a life partner, thanks to you, Airik. You bastard."

"I was going to ask you to marry me, but I just feel like it would be a big mistake."

"Did you foresee that?" she spat out sarcastically.

I tried to remain calm. "I don't need a vision to tell me the future of our relationship. Do you think we have problems?"

"Of course we do, but I wish you had broken up with me earlier. We're both so close to The Akuna. Now I have to go looking for a mate all over again. It's a pain."

I gazed at her compassionately, wondering how I had ever thought that she and I might be a good match. She was right, though. We were both getting uncomfortably close to The Akuna.

"Sornalee, you're exaggerating. You have at least half a year still. You know there's a two-year minimum for people to choose their life partners. That gives you two years and six months."

"I know," she said, her eyes tearing up a little. "But I have always dreamed of getting married on my Akuna. You know? Like in the story books?"

I sighed.

"I'm sorry, Sorna. I really am."

"So am I," she said, not looking angry anymore. "I'll have a hard time finding a life partner who's as good looking as you are, Airik."

"And as rich," I added as a joke. She took it seriously.

"That too."

I shook my head. Good thing I dodged that bullet. What had I been thinking?

I walked into a large room filled with Recorders. The area was a disorganized mess. They sat, stood, walked on treadmills, or wandered randomly at will, all while extracting necessary information from their assigned Precogs. I spotted Miroll in a corner throwing a ball against the wall as she talked to another of her Precogs.

I made my way over to her. Recorders who caught my eye waved to me. I waved back and smiled at them though this level of interaction wasn't necessary for someone of my rank.

I rubbed my third eye, which tingled. For thousands of years, the spot had been recognized in spirituality as a place of great significance in the body. We now knew better. The cortex of intuition and precognition — the part of the brain directly beneath the third eye on the forehead — could receive visions of the future.

As I walked to her, Miroll held up one finger, and I patiently waited for her to finish. After a few minutes, she pressed the communications unit behind her ear.

"Hello, Director Buhari. What happened to the Precog?" she asked. I rolled my eyes, still irritated that I had not received the complete vision.

"My girlfriend walked in and startled me out of it, Miroll."

"Oh," she said, looking uncomfortable.

Too much information, I supposed. Being the Director of the Precog Division was a great honor and something I had been striving for my whole life, but it also kept me apart from my people. The separation wasn't something I had anticipated or desired. I pushed my personal thoughts out of my head and focused on the vision.

"Did you pinpoint the location yet?"

She nodded, tapping her temple. I knew she was activating her personal computation device. It was an ocular implant used by knowledge workers, allowing her to see a computer screen and access information from huge mainframe computers, all private to her line of sight. She stared at something I couldn't see for a moment and blinked a few times.

"Here it is," she said. "It's on Earth." She looked at me in dismay.

"Earth?" I couldn't believe it.

The planet was one of the most backward and economically disadvantaged in the galaxy. Most civilized species ignored the humans. If we deigned to notice them, it was usually because some do-gooder decided they needed charity or one of them broke a law.

I didn't know why they were allowed to join the Union. Their civilization was barely ready for interstellar contact. In my opinion, they had pockets of social unrest that should have prevented their acceptance. That planet had problems to fix.

"Earth," she confirmed. "Director, have you ever had a vision of someone off-planet before?"

I shook my head. "Never."

"You ranked her significance at eleven?"

"I did at the time. I'm not sure anymore."

"Let's debrief you and see if we can find out more about this Earther."

"Okay," I said. We walked through the buzzing room, and Miroll pulled out a debriefing checklist, a bunch of questions designed to draw out more information about a Precog vision.

"When you think about the woman, the subject of your vision, how do you feel?" Miroll asked.

It was a standard question. I closed my eyes, trying to recapture the feeling of the Precog. When I opened my eyes, I felt my skin heating up, and I was thankful for my dark skin that hid my blush.

"Director?" Miroll said, confused by my hesitation. She repeated the question. "When you think about her, how do you feel?"

I thought momentarily about lying. Most Recorders were empaths, so there was no point in concealing the truth. She would know. It didn't matter whether she called me on it right now or not. She would have to note it on my file. In any event, my integrity was important to me. I would never jeopardize it by lying to prevent a momentary embarrassment in front of my Recorder.

I looked away from her and recited my feelings quickly.

"Love, happiness, and..." I hesitated. This was ridiculous. "Desire."

"Noted." That was the only thing she said, but when I glanced at her, she gave me a speculative gaze. "I will send you a full report in the morning, Director Buhari."

"Thank you, Miroll. Long life."

"Long life, Director."

When I looked back at her, she was reaching up to activate the communications unit behind her ear. There was another Precog coming in already.

As I stopped to put on my coat and hat before I headed out of the government building and back home, I thought about my vision. Why was I dreaming about a woman from Earth? Why did I think she was significant?

When was she going to die?

CHAPTER 3

QUINN

I wanted to scream. My body wouldn't obey me. I couldn't move, but I was aware of everything happening around me. The pain in my neck spread down my torso, past my thighs, and all the way down to my toes. I didn't know what drug they used on me. I just knew it hurt, and I couldn't move or open my eyes.

"Pick her up and let's get out of here. Nobody inside noticed her collapse."

"What about the old man in the car?"

"Michael's covering him."

I felt someone pick me up and toss me over their shoulder.

Since they hadn't mentioned Dad again, I assumed he was still in the car. That was a bright spot. I didn't want him risking his life for me. I realized now that it was bad enough when I dragged him into my mess with the Sons of the Heavenly Father. I was a grown woman. I should have handled it on my own and left my Dad out of it.

But that was a moot point right now. I had bigger things to worry about, like how to avoid being their next victim.

If they took me away, they were going to kill me. I wondered how they would do it. Burn me, probably. At the stake. It would be funny if I weren't going to die. I couldn't do anything to stop it. I had to see what was going to happen. I could try to save myself when I had control of my body again.

Unless they never let you wake up.

The thought was chilling, and I hadn't considered it before. What if they had drugged me enough to keep me conscious but unable to fight back. And what if they were going to tie me to a stake and burn me alive?

I began to panic. As different thoughts raced through my mind, I felt trapped, and I knew I would make myself crazy. I need to calm down. But what could I do?

Nothing. Nothing at all.

I felt frustration and anger rising in me. The futility of my wasted life hit me like a slap in the face. I realized I had spent over half of my life hiding, and I hadn't truly lived at all.

Now I was going to die.

Rage filled me, and my face began to get hot. Maybe blood was rushing to my head from being carried upside-down.

"Hey, man. There's something wrong with her," the man holding me said, stopping suddenly.

"What do you mean?"

"Feel her skin."

Someone touched my hand.

"It's hot. She feels like she's on fire."

"Maybe the witch is sick."

"She won't be sick for long. Don't worry about it. Just keep carrying her. We're almost to the car. When we get where we're going, she's not going to worry about having a fever."

I should have been afraid, I suppose. But I wasn't. I was pissed. I couldn't believe this was happening to me. I felt like I was going to boil over with rage, especially since I couldn't unleash my fury on anyone.

"Something weird's going on, Rick. She's sweltering."

"You can't handle a girl all by yourself? Give her to me."

I felt them transfer me, and I got madder and madder. I was little more than an object to these punks.

"You're right. She's scorching hot."

Finally, I couldn't stand it anymore. In my mind, I screamed my frustration. My voice never made a sound, but I knew the energy went somewhere.

"She's burning me!" I felt someone drop me on the ground. "I can't carry her like this."

I could feel the night air against the skin of my hands. It didn't feel cold at all. Someone touched my hand.

"Ow! Look at this, Rick. My skin is smoking."

"She is a witch. Here come the cops the cops. We'll have to come back for her another time."

"No way, man. I'm not coming back. They can send a lone assassin to kill her. I'm not risking my life to deal with a real witch."

I heard their footsteps moving away from me. Doors slammed. A vehicle's tires squealed as it sped away.

Some time later I heard my Dad's voice. "Here she is."

I wanted to warn him that something weird was happening, and he shouldn't touch me. I still couldn't move. When he picked me up, he didn't complain about me being hot, or anything like that.

Weird.

I was carried back in an unknown direction. I hoped I was back in my Dad's car. After a long time, my Dad spoke again.

"Phillip, thank God. Please help me carry her in." Phillip was Dad's best friend.

"Justin, what happened?"

"Someone attacked us. No, that's not right. Someone attacked her. I was tied up. That's why I couldn't reach her in time. They drugged her, and she's knocked out."

Not knocked out, I wanted to say, but my body was still unresponsive.

"But what happened?" Phillip asked as they laid me down on the couch. We were probably at Phillip's apartment.

I listened as Dad told our entire story again. Right after they shot me with a dart, another member of their group had tied Dad up in the car. Someone from the police station came out when they saw what was happening on the video feed. They drove off before the police could arrest them. The cops were still searching for my attackers. Dad had taken me to the hospital. They ran tests on me, but the doctor said I wasn't in any danger and just needed to sleep the drug off.

I felt Dad tucking me in with a blanket. Phillip suggested they let me sleep. When they went into the kitchen, I couldn't hear any more. Knowing that I was safe, I let myself fall asleep.

The next morning, my mind felt normal when I woke up. My body felt like I had run a marathon yesterday without any training. My muscles ached, and my movements were leaden. I sat up on the couch but didn't have the nerve to go any farther. While I was still sitting there, trying to find the courage to get off the couch, my father entered.

"Quinn! I'm so glad you're okay. How do you feel? Can you move at all? Does it hurt?"

I put my hand to my neck and felt a bandage where the dart pierced my skin.

"I'm okay, Dad. It's all right. Don't worry. I can move. I'm just sore. I know everything that happened last night."

"I thought you were knocked out," he said, looking puzzled.

"Someone hit me with a dart in the neck. My body felt like it was knocked out, and I looked out of it, but I was still conscious."

"Do you know why they left you?"

I dropped my eyes. "I have an idea."

"What, Quinn? What is it?"

"I think it had something to do with my visions."

"Your visions. What do you mean? Wasn't that why they wanted to take you?"

"I was getting angry. I was furious I was going to die because of these stupid, bigoted jerks. I felt myself getting hot…"

"Like a fever?"

"At first I thought my face was feeling hot because I was in an awkward position. But then something odd happened."

My dad looked at me. He was interested in what I had to say but wasn't judging me.

"I started burning them."

My dad stared at me. "That sounds like an extraordinary gift."

"I know. It was like all my anger converted into heat. They got scared, and then the cops showed up."

"My goodness, Quinn."

"I'm even more of a freak than we thought."

He sighed. "You have to leave Earth," he said slowly. His head and shoulders slumped forward.

"What?" I said, glancing up sharply. "I'm not going away."

"Yes, Quinn. You are. It's too dangerous."

"But you need me. And we can't afford it. And I can't *leave*." The thought filled me with fear and anguish. I had never considered leaving our home planet or my dad. He was my only family. I had never separated from him.

"You can and you will," he said. "Something broke inside me when I saw those men attack you. If they hurt you or kill you, I will never forgive myself. I've been trying to protect you and your gift for years. I've failed."

"You have taken good care of me, Dad."

He held up his hand.

"No, I haven't, Quinn. It's been a terrible life. I want better for you."

I stared at him with tears in my eyes. He had never spoken to me so insistently or so firmly. I knew he meant what he said.

"Even if I agreed with you, how would I do it?"

"Phillip has heard about a company called TerraMates. They can get you out of here, and you'll get some money. Best of all, it's only for a year."

"What's only for a year?" I said, feeling suspicious. "Hang on a second. It's called TerraMates? As in..." I trailed off, not wanting to put my suspicion into words.

My father looked uncomfortable and nodded.

"It's a mail-order bride company. They arrange marriages to aliens. That's how we'll move you off the planet."

"We are not to be used as an escape from Earth, Miss Maloney. I hope you understand that," said Mrs. Lynch, the owner of TerraMates. She looked at me slightly disapprovingly, tapping her well-manicured fingernail on the desk. I was filling out some forms, and she was reviewing my answers.

I looked up from the computer. I had to supply an endless amount of information about myself and the qualities I looked for in a mate. In the 'other' box, I had made sure to check 'must be tolerant of mental abilities'.

"Of course not," I said, feeling my guts clench but looking her straight in the eye. "Why would you think I was doing that?"

"You must admit, Miss Maloney, that your behavior looks suspicious."

"I don't admit any such thing. I'm excited to be going off-world, of course. But it's because I'm curious to meet my husband and learn about an alien culture. I wouldn't have even mentioned the Sons of the Heavenly Father. There was a question about my interactions with the law and I thought it meant..."

"The wording is 'problems'. You didn't have an issue with the law. The people who attacked you did."

"Right. Yes, I suppose."

"I see your altercation happened quite recently. Which is why I will repeat myself. We are not for escaping."

"And I'm not using you that way. I honestly have a desire to travel, and I'm getting older, Mrs. Lynch. It's time I put down some roots." All true enough, though maybe not in the way she interpreted them.

She stared at me. I calmly gazed back. I wouldn't flinch. I was not going to be intimidated by her iron gray coiffeur, power suit, and hawk-like gaze. I thought I was going to have to look away, but to my surprise, she glanced down at her computer first.

An unexpected feeling of relief and victory shot through me. I guessed Mrs. Lynch didn't let many people stare her down. I smiled a little and kept filling in the form. She moved on to a different topic of conversation.

"Of course, as you would have read in the contract, you do not have to have sexual intercourse with your husband, unless both of you decide you want to."

I nodded. I wasn't going to be a whore. This idea was bad enough. I didn't need to prostitute myself as well.

"There will be periodic check-ups to confirm everything is going well, and there is no abuse on either side. We will send your credits as soon as we receive validation of your marriage certificate. If you wish to divorce after a year, you have only to contact us. We will assist with the process."

"Is there a long wait to get the divorce?" I said. I wondered if I would have to stay married for much longer than a year.

She looked surprised by my question. "No, dear. We don't get many wives coming back and asking for a divorce."

"Are you serious?" I said, my voice incredulous. "I don't believe it."

"Miss Maloney, we run an excellent service here. To the best of our abilities, women are matched with their perfect mates."

I laughed at her hubris.

"Can you predict true love?" I said. My voice had a mocking tone, but part of me thought about my ability to see the future. If I could predict what could happen, why couldn't they?

"That is unnecessary. We have extremely sophisticated matching algorithms. In general, the women who come here are not looking for true love." She had a way of speaking that made her words drip with condescension. "They are looking for a good man who can provide them with companionship and financial support. The women who come to us are practical, Miss Maloney. We have a 2 percent divorce rate."

2 percent? I didn't believe it. But if she was lying, she wasn't going to change her story if I asked her about it. And if she wasn't...Well, that didn't make sense to me. Why wouldn't the women put in their time, grab their money, file for divorce and move on with their life?

Mrs. Lynch sighed.

"Based on the surveys that are filled out by the women who stay married..." She stared at a report but then looked up and met my eyes. "97 percent say they have come to love their husbands, Miss Maloney."

I rolled my eyes. I wasn't going to love mine. I would put in my year, get the money to send back to Dad, and get a divorce. As soon as my tour of duty was over I was going to find my real true love. I would track him down and save both of us from death by a tree. I had a vague sense of how far into the future events would happen. The vision felt like about a year from now. I had time.

I had never been able to save anyone from my visions before, but I had not tried as hard as I could. This time, I was going to do it. He was the man I would love. I was not going to let him die.

CHAPTER 4

AIRIK

"Airik, you're late. *Again.*"

"Hi Mom," I said, kissing her on the forehead. "I told you I was working late."

"You're always working late."

"It's important. Even more important now than before."

"I know you've been working towards this goal since you were a boy. But your life can't be entirely focused on work. There's family, too. And a wife in your future, I hope." She had a tentative look on her face as if she was expecting me to get mad at her.

"Mother, I know that The Akuna is coming up soon. My birthday is in two weeks. Even if I could forget it, you wouldn't let me."

"We just want you to be happy, Airik."

"Yeah, happy. And you don't want to be the parents whose son lost his job because he hadn't married by the Akuna. That wouldn't make me socially acceptable."

"Airik, stop. We want this for you. Did your boss threaten you about your job?"

"He did. It's the law. He has to uphold it. If I'm not married by my birthday, they will have to fire me. I'm the

40

only Director of the Precog Division who wasn't already married when they took the position."

"Because you were smart, intuitive, and brilliant. That's why they promoted you despite your age."

I smiled. My mom had a way of making me feel good about myself, even if I was a loser.

"Right now, I don't fulfill the requirements of the job. Everyone in a senior government position has to be married by their Akuna. It's a royal decree."

She tsked.

"We don't even have a monarchy anymore. Why hasn't anyone got rid of that stupid rule? Don't they make exceptions for people?"

"Most people get married by their Akuna. I'm a terrible exception."

"Airik, you could still get married. I know some lovely women. Your father does, too. Everyone seems to know a girl who is perfect for you."

"Everyone's wrong," I said with a frown. "I had a vision, Mom."

"About who?"

"It was about a woman I'm going to fall in love with."

"Really?" She sounded excited now.

"Yeah, but don't start inviting people yet. I saw her death." For the first time, I heard how heavy my voice sounded. I realized my vision had been bothering me more than I thought.

"Was it death from old age, at home, by your side?" she asked tentatively.

"No. I think she will die soon. I don't know what exactly happens because Sornalee interrupted me."

"We all knew that you weren't going to marry her. She's such an airhead," she muttered.

"Why didn't you tell me?" I had broken up with Sorna right after her interruption. I hadn't been able to find out how the woman died or when it would happen. I was furious with my ditzy former girlfriend. Mom was right when she said marrying her would be a mistake.

"Would you have listened to me?"

"Probably not," I conceded. "It certainly wasn't Sorna in my vision."

"But this woman," my mom said, seizing on the important point. "The one you're going to love. If you've foreseen her death, you can save her. The Precog Division will rescue her, just like they take care of everyone else on Koccoran."

"Not everyone, Mom."

"Almost everyone, Airik. You can save her, too."

"There's a problem." I hesitated because I knew how she would react.

"What problem could there possibly be? You have a job. Get the Ground Team moving. You've got to make sure that girl lives."

"I don't think the Ground Team operates this far out," I said, reluctant to tell her.

"Why not?"

"Because she dies on Earth."

"Earth?"

"She's a human."

"A human?" I winced when I heard the shock and dismay in her tone. I supposed acceptance by the family wasn't going to happen. I hadn't even met this girl yet, and might never meet her. She may have been killed with a poisoned dart already.

I was saved from an uncomfortable conversation when my brother walked into the room.

"Did I hear you talking about The Akuna, Airik?"

I nodded.

"I've got the perfect solution to your problem."

"What's that?" If I didn't humor him, he might sulk for weeks, and I didn't need new drama.

43

"Have you ever heard of TerraMates? They'll arrange your marriages for you, with an alien. You get married for a year, and if you want to get divorced, your time is up and you're free to move on. The women get an exorbitant amount of credits for moving halfway across the galaxy and marrying a stranger. You get the wife you need with no commitment and, more importantly, no lovey-dovey issues. You know, the stuff you hate in a relationship." I saw my mother frown out of the corner of my eye, but I ignored her.

"It's complicated now."

"Are you talking about the dream girl from your visions?"

"You overheard me?"

"Sorry, but you're not in a closed room here. If you wanted privacy, you should have gone into the den."

I shrugged. It didn't matter. My mother knew already. Everyone else would know soon enough, even perfect strangers.

"Well, this is what you do. Get an arranged marriage to satisfy your superiors. It's a ridiculous and outdated law. Divorce this woman after a year and find your true love."

"Divorce is unacceptable," I said.

"Unacceptable," he said, looking at me like I was stupid. "Not illegal."

He had a point, but it was still a dumb idea.

"That's ridiculous, Kartar. I'm not going to marry a stranger."

"Would you rather lose your job and everything you've worked for?" he said in disbelief.

When he put it that way, it was a rather compelling argument. I felt myself start to capitulate.

"Airik, let me help you out with this. I'll go through the process for you. You'll just have to sign on the dotted line. There are interviews you'll have to do yourself, but I'll do everything possible. Consider it my birthday present to you."

I felt my mind scrambling for other options. There were none. I was running out of time. This solution would give me a wife. No questions asked, no strings attached. I didn't like to get serious with my girlfriends. An arranged marriage was the least serious relationship I could imagine. It was more like a business deal.

Besides, I didn't have a choice, as he had pointed out. My career was everything to me. I wouldn't jeopardize it for something as stupid as The Akuna.

"Okay, Kartar. I didn't know what I was going to do."

"No problem, big brother. You've helped me out more times than I can count. I owe you."

Just like that, I was getting a wife.

I stood in the transporter room, feeling more nervous than I ever had before. A woman on that ship was going to be my wife. Even if we were only married for a year, it was an enormous commitment. And one taken seriously on Koccoran. I was going to get married today.

I had never met my fiancee.

I heard the unmistakable sound of a transporter beaming in and looked up to see a beautiful woman shimmer into solid form.

She wasn't too tall. I estimated she would come up to my chin. But she was willowy, with long limbs, graceful fingers, and a delicate oval face. Her hair was jet-black and loose, reaching to her waist. She gazed at me with piercing blue eyes. No one on Koccoran had blue eyes. For a moment, I wondered where my brother had found her. Then I pushed the thought out of my mind. I didn't want to bring preconceived notions to the table. I wanted to form my opinion of my wife.

The last thing I noticed about her physical appearance was that her skin was so pale it was almost translucent, and completely without a blemish. No one had skin that color on Koccoran, either. I found myself longing to touch it. Was it as smooth as it looked?

I didn't realize I was staring at her, and I struggled to find my voice.

"Welcome." I swallowed. "My name is Airik Buhari."

She looked blankly at me.

"You don't speak Galactic Standard?" I said with a frown. What kind of a marriage agency was TerraMates? Standard was a language spoken everywhere in the galaxy. Eventually, with all the millions of languages in use as populations from different planets met and interacted, it was necessary to adopt a language everyone would use that was common to all worlds.

After the Union of Planets had passed the Language Standardization Act, all the planets that were a part of the Union were required to adopt it within twenty years. That was fifty years ago. I thought by this point everyone spoke Standard. If she didn't, I was starting to wonder about her home planet.

"Oh, no. I speak Standard. And English."

"English. An ancient language," I said. "Interesting. I have a fascination with ancient languages." I made a mental note to work on my English.

I was curious where she was from, but I didn't ask. Kartar hadn't given me any info on her and it was better that I make up my mind about her without any preconceptions.

I held out my hands crossed at the wrist. She looked down at them, and an expression of panic flitted across her face. She rubbed nervously at a bright red scar on her neck. It was in the shape of a circle. I hadn't noticed it before because her long hair hid it.

"It's a greeting on Koccoran. Hold out your hands like mine."

She nodded and crossed her arms. I smiled. "You must be Quinn?"

"Yes, that's me," she said. "I'm sorry. I'm not usually such an idiot. But I'm afraid I lost the folder containing information about Koccoran culture and everything about you. I'm flying blind here."

There was a folder? I hadn't received anything. I wondered if Kartar had forgotten to give it to me, or if he had done it on purpose.

"Me too. I never even got a folder to lose."

She looked as uncomfortable as I felt.

"Shall we go? We'll be traveling to the next town over, where I live. We'll be getting married today. You know we have to get married within 24 hours, right?"

"Right." She paused. "Are we having a religious ceremony?" She looked upset at the thought, and I wondered why.

"No. Marriage is a civil or social custom and is run by the government. We have no religion on Koccoran."

"That's perfect," she said. Quinn was more relieved than I would have expected. I gave her a forced smile and turned to leave the transporter room, wishing the transport attendant long life.

I knew the attendant was a telepath. She had a strange look on her face as I left. She had probably never seen me tongue-tied. Now that I thought about it, I don't remember having problems speaking like this before. I hoped it wouldn't continue. It would be a long year if we were going to be this uncomfortable together.

We had only just met; I was determined to give us a chance. I needed to marry her. I didn't care if we sat in silence for an entire year. She was the reason I would keep my career.

We arrived at the garage, and I found some warm outerwear that had arrived for her. TerraMates provided it.

"Here you go. These are your outdoor clothes."

Quinn stared at them with mild distaste in her eyes. "I have to change what I'm wearing?"

"You don't know anything about Koccoran, do you?"

She swallowed and started to shiver. It was cool in the garage because the door was always opening and shutting, letting people and air into the Transporter Center.

"It's below zero outside," I said. "You need to protect yourself." She didn't move. "Maybe you didn't know to bring your gear?" I said, pulling on snow pants over my regular pants.

"I don't have any gear," she said, slowly.

"You don't? How is that possible?"

"At home, there's no snow. It never gets colder than twenty-one degrees."

"Wow," I said, feeling worried. "You're in for a bit of shock. We're in the middle of winter right now."

She looked upset, but then she lifted her chin. "I'll be all right. It's just cold. Right?"

I gave her another tight smile. "That's right."

I wasn't smiling on the inside. This was not a positive development. I should have told Kartar to put down something about the weather or the environment. Now I was stuck with a fragile flower who wouldn't be able to handle the cold. I didn't like coddling people.

She pulled on the clothes awkwardly. I noticed the red coat looked stunning with her black hair and fair skin. She was truly beautiful.

"If you pull your socks over your regular pants before you put on the snow pants, they won't ride up. Just a little tip for next time."

"Thanks," she said. I waited until she finished dressing, then led her through the garage to the small door that led outside.

As we stepped out the exit, the wind hit us in the face with some snow that had blown off the roof. She flinched in shock. I looked at her with pity and concern.

"Pull your scarf up, Quinn. It will protect your face."

She nodded and clumsily pulled her scarf up without taking off her gloves. I walked over to the nearest snow car. It was similar to vehicles I had seen on planets where they didn't have snow ten months of the year. Instead of wheels, it had tracks to go over the snow and travel between cities. During the brief, two-month summer, smaller self-driving cars were used for transportation.

The driver opened his door. "Hey buddy, we need a ride to Nivan."

"I can do that," he said. "Hop in."

I opened the door and let Quinn climb in first. An hour later, we were in the small town of Nivan. During the walk from the parking lot to the wedding location, Quinn struggled to move in her big boots. It had snowed heavily yesterday. The snow removal division was still in the process of getting all the sidewalks cleared. They hadn't got to this one yet, and it was up to our knees.

Finally, we got to the door, and I opened it, holding it for her. I didn't miss the sigh of relief that she let out when she felt the warmth inside.

"Come over here and take your extra clothes off," I said as we stepped through the second set of double doors. To our left was a coat room. We removed our boots and set them on a mat. The snow would melt and drain into a shallow trough underneath the footwear. On the wall, there were hooks for hanging up our snow pants and coats.

I motioned to a device that looked like a long radiator but had loops pointing up on the top. "Put your gloves, hat, and scarf here to dry. The loops heat up and dry off your clothing. The theory is that they will be warm and dry before you go out again into the terrible weather."

"Nice," she said. She put her gloves and hat each over one of the loops, then wound her scarf around a couple of them. I felt entranced when I watched her movements. She was lovely and elegant. When she looked up at me after she finished putting all her outdoor clothes away, her crystal clear blue eyes ensnared me. I couldn't seem to look away.

I wondered if she felt it as well. The moment stretched, but she looked away first.

"We should go this way," I said, turning away from her. Why did I feel guilty? Quinn was going to be a temporary wife. My true love was somewhere far away on a backward planet. I had to nurture the hope that she would be safe until I found her. I wasn't sure how far into the future my vision was. Perhaps it was a year or more away, and I could still find her and save her. I had no business getting interested in another woman.

We walked through the large entrance and into a corridor. I turned into a room whose nameplate read:

Maloney-Buhari Wedding

Quinn gazed at the sign and read the words slowly. There was no time for hesitation.

"Come on," I said, taking her hand. She looked at me in surprise. "We have to keep up appearances. My mother and my brother are the only ones who know you're from TerraMates."

"Oh." Her eyes were big.

"Can you pretend you like me? Hopefully, you will, soon enough."

She laughed then and shook her head.

"I like you, Airik. I won't have to pretend."

The words warmed my heart but made me feel guilty at the same time. Even if I wasn't getting involved with her, wasn't it was a good idea to like my wife?

"I like you too, Quinn," I said. "Ready?"

"Ready."

I opened the door and lifted my head high as we walked into a room packed with over a hundred people. I heard Quinn's shocked gasp. To her credit, she kept her smile firmly in place.

"I thought you said we were meeting your family," she said out of the side of her mouth.

"Yes," I said as we walked forward.

"What are all these people doing here?"

53

I turned and smiled at her. A genuine smile for the first time.

"This is my family."

CHAPTER 5

QUINN

By my estimate, Airik had about a million people in his family. It appeared they were all coming to my wedding. I had already met about twenty of them, but I couldn't remember a single name. I was starting to freak out.

My Dad was on another planet. I was on my own in a sea of people.

Airik hadn't let go of my hand. It was a small measure of comfort that made me feel secure. Occasionally, we had to release each other when our wrists crossed, but then he would take my cold hand in his again as we made our way through the crowd.

I wished again that I hadn't mislaid the folder about my prospective husband. I couldn't believe I lost it. I had considered asking Mrs. Lynch for another one, but I couldn't work up the courage. I was worried she would think I wasn't responsible enough to be a mail-order bride.

The truth was, Mrs. Lynch terrified me. She was a harpy. I should have asked her despite my misgivings. Now I knew nothing about these aliens and their culture. What if I offended someone by accident?

And I wished Airik had told me ahead of time that I was going to have to act like we were in love. But when could he have told me? I just arrived on the planet. He let me know as soon as he could, I guess. And I supposed it wasn't a big deal. It was merely another part of our sham marriage.

I didn't know why he wanted to marry me. Keeping up appearances seemed important, so I would do that for him.

I meant it when I had said that I liked him. He seemed kind. There was something reassuring about him. He projected confidence and calm. It seemed he was usually in charge and knew how to put people at ease.

If I could only get through this day, I was sure I could get through another year. Airik introduced me to his closest family members. I met his mother, his father, his three brothers and two sisters. My mind started melting when friends said hello, followed by favorite cousins, aunts, uncles. By the time we finished lunch, I was exhausted.

There were two full days to rest on the space station before the shuttle left for Koccoran. I was over my jet lag. There wasn't anything physically wrong with me.

But I hadn't been around people for years. Mostly my life was Dad and me, especially at the end when we were always looking over our shoulders. I stayed at home alone all day and spent time with my Dad, or trusted friends would come over. I hadn't been in a group this size for a long, long time. And frankly, it was making me nervous.

"Are you ready to go back to the room?" Airik said when he noticed I was finished eating.

"Yes, please."

He said our good-byes for us and we headed up to the hotel room. When we arrived, I collapsed on the couch. He asked me if everything was all right.

"I'm okay. I'm just tired. I haven't been around this many people in a long time. Probably not since I was in school, so it's overwhelming along with everything else."

"I'm sorry, Quinn. We'll have a few hours to rest but then the wedding and the reception are coming, along with more crowds."

"I know. That's okay. Of course you want your family here. I didn't know there would be so many of them. I don't know anything about you, do I?"

"Right," he said, looking worried for a moment. His expression evened out. "We'll get to know each other."

"Yes, we will," I said. My voice had more conviction than I felt. Right now Airik was a complete stranger. I thought I would never know him any better than I did right now. It seemed like an impossible task.

"It's a suite," he said, walking to a door and opening it to reveal a bedroom. "Do you want to sleep for a while? I have some work to do, but I can get it done at the table."

"That sounds wonderful." I sank gratefully onto the bed and pulled off my thick sweater. Underneath I had on a pink T-shirt. "Thanks, Airik, for being understanding."

I looked up, and he was staring at me in a way that made my body tingle. I felt my heart rate accelerate, and my breath came more quickly. Our eyes were locked. His gaze felt like foreplay.

I hadn't been in a relationship since high school. There was one guy that had been a loner. He was an artist and different from everyone else, like me. One night, down by the river, we had both lost our virginity.

Another guy seduced me at the bar one night when I was twenty-two. We went home together, and he disappeared before I woke up. But there hadn't been anyone since then.

I hadn't wanted anyone, until now. I swallowed.

"Rest well, Quinn," he said. When he spoke, I imagined a kiss on my lips.

"Thank you," I said.

He nodded and left.

I fell back on the bed. My body tingled. I felt alive for the first time in years. What was going on? And what about the man I was supposed to be in love with in a year's time? How could I consider anything with Airik when my mystery man was still out there in the universe?

I briefly wondered if it could be Airik. But what were the chances I would have a vision of my true love, and he would turn out to be the man I had already married? Slim to none.

It felt strange to be panting over Airik when I knew there was a different someone out there for me. It was almost like cheating. But if I hadn't had a vision, I wouldn't know anything about the man from the future, and I wouldn't have any misgivings about having sex with my husband.

What about all the people a person dates before they find the person they want to marry? Does that make them disloyal to a person from their future? Of course not. When they're dating the person, they don't know what's going to happen.

Did it even matter? We weren't going to be jumping into bed together. We would get to know each other first and then if it seemed like a good idea, something might happen. I remembered how it felt locking eyes with him halfway across the room, and my body disagreed with my mind. My body didn't see a need for a getting-to-know period.

It wanted him. And that was that.

I sighed, pulling my pants off and crawling into bed in my T-shirt and underwear. All my philosophical thoughts would have to wait until later. I needed a nap if I was going to be able to face my wedding and reception. I sighed at the thought.

How was I going to live through the rest of this day?

Have a nap, I counseled myself. *Everything will look better when you wake up.*

I curled up on my side and quickly fell fast asleep.

I woke slowly, aware that there was a foreign scent in my vicinity. It was a little spicy, a little exotic and it made me weak with need. I had been dreaming of Airik. The content of my dreams made me blush. My heart was still pounding because I had woken up as we were about to become intimate.

"Quinn?" I heard Airik's voice calling softly from above me. Wait a second. He was sitting next to me on my bed. My pulse raced.

"Quinn, your face is changing color. Do you feel okay?"

I didn't answer immediately. I was too embarrassed. I didn't think he had much experience with fair-skinned people. On Koccoran, it would be impossible to tell if people were blushing or not because they were many shades darker than my pale skin.

Eyes closed, I responded to him. "I'm blushing."

"Oh," he said. "Why? Am I making you uncomfortable?"

Was his voice huskier than before? I felt myself getting wet. This would not do. I needed to keep our relationship platonic. Didn't I?

"No," I said, finally opening my eyes.

"You seemed fast asleep. I'm sorry to wake you up, but it's time to get dressed for the wedding," he said.

"Okay," I said. I didn't want to sit up because my nipples were hard and would be obvious in my tight shirt when the blanket fell off of me.

He smiled and leaned over me, kissing my forehead.

The moment his lips touched me, I had a flash of images race through my mind too fast for me to grasp. He pulled away in surprise, examining me as if trying to comprehend something.

I sat up and moved back away from him. "What was that?" I asked.

"What was what? Did you experience something?"

I stared at him.

I couldn't tell him I saw visions. Hiding was ingrained in my soul by now. What if he didn't understand? Maybe he was like the Sons of the Heavenly Father back on Earth? I had concealed my abilities for years. I could certainly hide them for one more.

"It was nothing." I looked away. "I thought I heard something, but I was wrong."

I glanced up at him and was surprised to see him give me a speculative look. Was he trying to figure me out? He shook his head slowly as if dismissing whatever he had been thinking.

"I see," he said, rising to his feet. "You will find a wedding gown in the closet. It is a traditional dress. My sister will be along shortly to help you put it on."

He headed for the door, and I called after him. "I don't need any help. I can dress myself."

He looked back over his shoulder in a way that could only be called distracting.

"Trust me. The dress requires assistance, and Neesa wants to get to know you."

I relented. The last thing I wanted was to get lost trying to wear alien fashion. Neesa was one of his relatives that had seemed nice. I remembered her.

"Okay, maybe you're right," I said, getting up.

He went very still, and I froze too. Our attraction was back, and he was still far away from me. How would it feel when I was in his arms?

"What is it?" I couldn't help asking.

"You're very beautiful. Your pictures didn't do you justice."

I smiled. "You're easy on the eyes, too," I said, borrowing an expression from my father.

He certainly was.

He was tall, not too broad, but strong. He wore conservative clothes, but I was sure that I would find a well-muscled body underneath. The thought made me flush. His hair was black and very short. His mocha skin gave me shivers. I wanted to see what it looked like alongside my pale body.

I had already lost myself in his chocolate brown eyes several times. His dark goatee made him look distinguished and handsome. His lips, though, had me mesmerized. They were full and sexy. The only thing I wanted to do was press my own against them.

What was I thinking?

I had just met this guy. How could I want him so much? But it had been a long time since I had found a desirable partner. Perhaps I was starved for love...or maybe it was something else. I had to admit I was powerfully attracted to Airik, more than any guy I had ever met. He seemed to want me, too, if the tent in his pants was any indication. He turned, finally, as though he had to wrench himself away from me.

"I'll see you when you've dressed, Quinn," he said, passing his sister on his way out of my room.

She looked at him, looked at me, and raised her eyebrows. "For an arranged marriage, you guys seem quite interested in each other."

My mouth dropped open. "I thought you didn't know."

"Don't worry, nobody else knows. But Kartar never could keep a secret from me. I knew something was up. I made him tell me everything."

"Does Airik know that you know?"

"Nah, I'll tell him later."

I nodded.

"So, there's some chemistry between you two?" she asked, grinning at me.

"Yeah. I guess there is."

"That's good. You'll need it tonight."

I supposed she was referring to any required kisses at the reception. "Should we get this dress on?"

"We should, but put this underwear on first." She handed me crotchless panties and a bra that could be unbuttoned to allow my breasts to burst out.

"Wait a second. What kind of kink are you aliens into on this planet?" I said. The words popped out before I could stop them. I clapped my hand over my mouth, then took it off to apologize. "I'm sorry. I didn't mean that."

"No, no," she laughed. "You have a right to know what the interesting underwear is about. I'm here to explain everything."

"Explain away."

"You've noticed that we live in a cold climate. A long time ago, we lived in cabins that could be quite chilly. Sometimes people didn't take their clothes off for weeks at a time."

I wrinkled my nose. "No offense, but that sounds pretty gross."

"I know. It was my ancestors, not me. If you ever visit one of the historical cabins during the winter, you'll know why they didn't change. You wouldn't have, either."

"You're probably right," I said.

"They would sleep in their clothes as well. But newlyweds have certain needs."

"Okay." I knew where this was going now.

"And they weren't about to take off all their clothes in the bitter cold to fulfill those needs, no matter how urgent their desires."

"Of course not."

"They created underwear that would allow easy access to a woman's body."

I swallowed hard as I imagined Airik having easy access to my body.

"Sounds brilliant," I said.

"Exactly. The newlyweds could fulfill their needs whenever they wanted to. The women wore blouses that buttoned in the front and skirts. The men could always pull it out when they needed to."

I laughed.

"That's where the traditional underwear comes from."

"Okay. I'll just put it on then," I said, going into the bathroom.

"Here," she said, tossing me a ball of silk. "Put the slip on too."

When I came out, she had the dress ready for me to put on. I stepped into it from the top. As she had already indicated, the top half buttoned up for easy access.

It was like a princess dress. The blue shade happened to match my eyes exactly. My shoulders were bare. The sleeves were long and covered my entire arm. The bodice was tight and highlighted my narrow waist. The skirt fell smoothly over my hips all the way to the floor. It covered my shoes and swished when I walked.

When I turned and saw myself in the mirror, I couldn't believe I was looking at myself. I had lived my entire life in jeans and T-shirts. My dad had never been good at feminine things. The sight of myself in the dress made me smile.

"Do you like it?" Neesa asked.

"Oh, yeah, I like," I said, grinning at her.

"Now let's do your hair," she said.

We worked together and put it up in a bun at the back of my head. She attached a golden chain that went across my forehead and wrapped around the bun — a flat blue stone hung from the chain in the center of my forehead over my third eye. By the time we finished, I didn't even recognize myself.

"Wow," Neesa said, as I turned to her. "You look amazing, Quinn. Airik won't be able to resist you."

I didn't know what to say to that. I was saved by Neesa bustling me out the door and downstairs to a waiting room. As we crossed the lobby, there was an unfamiliar man that was watching me. It made me feel uncomfortable, but I ignored him. There must be weirdos on every planet.

We waited impatiently until the sound of a knock on the door made us both jump and then laugh.

"Come in," Neesa called.

"Hey ladies, it's time to start the show." It was Airik. When he caught sight of me, he was transfixed and spellbound. But I hardly noticed as I tried to wrap my head around how amazingly handsome and sexy he looked in his outfit.

Neesa looked back and forth between the two of us.

"Did we succeed in our mission, Quinn?" she said. I remembered that she was still in the room.

"I guess so," I said, having no idea what she meant.

"Mission? What mission?" Airik said, glancing at his little sister.

"The mission to overwhelm you with the beauty of your bride," she said, beaming at him.

"Oh yeah?" he said, looking back and devouring me with his eyes from head to toe. I felt myself blush again. "Mission accomplished."

CHAPTER 6

QUINN

I stifled another yawn. It had been a long day. It was nearly midnight. Airik and I sat at the front of the room at a long table, facing everyone. The table was up higher than the rest so everyone could see us, which increased my discomfort. I glanced down at my middle fingers.

I was married.

There was a silver band on each finger, studded with tiny blue stones matching the one on my forehead. An intricate pattern crisscrossed the metal. I loved them. Airik had two rings similar to mine. His were a copper color with the same etching. There were black stones sprinkled on his rings.

The ceremony had been strange, but the heart of it was familiar. It was the same as on Earth. We swore to love, honor, and take care of each other until death parted us. What else was there to say at a wedding?

I felt guilty swearing that when I wasn't planning on staying married to him. But I felt better when I promised myself that as long as we were married, I would honor the vows. I was making them in good faith. The marriage would just end sooner than eternity.

I unmistakably felt the presence of my future lover at the ceremony. I knew he was watching, somehow. There had been a profound sense of approval from his spirit. Maybe he was okay if I was with Airik for the year. Then I would divorce him and go and find my real true love.

When I was free, I would find the man with whom I was supposed to fall in love.

"Quinn?" Airik said, putting his hand over mine and making my heart skip a beat. "How are you?"

"I'm good. The ceremony was lovely. The rings are beautiful."

He dropped his head, looking a little bashful. "I'm glad you like them. I hoped you would."

The reception had stretched on with speeches, jokes, and people demanding we kiss each other. Airik gave me chaste kisses. They were almost pecks on the cheek. Maybe in their culture, those types of kisses were appropriate at a public event like this.

I had been so nervous that I drank several glasses of a beautiful pink drink that waiters kept setting in front of me. Eventually Airik cut me off, telling me that it was a potent alcohol and would make me drunk. By that time, it was too late. It was a good thing all I had to do was sit and look pretty. There wasn't any dancing.

As it turned out, it didn't matter why he was kissing me like I was his sister. I was having a hard enough time concentrating as it was, being drunk and horny. I didn't need him kissing me so passionately in front of all his family members that I forgot my name. I had a feeling he could kiss me like that.

I wondered if he would when we got back to our room. The thought made me shiver. I tried to focus on what he was saying.

"We can go now if you want to."

"Oh, can we? I'm exhausted."

"Yes, of course. Let's thank everyone and head up to our room."

"Okay," I said, my heart beating a little faster. Would he want to do anything when we arrived at our room?

I leaned on his arm as we said our thank yous and wished everyone a long life. We walked out of the conference room and into the lobby. I was surprised to notice that the man Neesa and I had seen earlier was still there. I could feel his eyes on me the whole time we were in the room. The way he was looking at me made my skin crawl.

Once we were in the elevator, I turned to Airik. "Do you know that man?"

"I don't," he said, frowning when he looked at me. "Why? Did he say something to you?"

"Not a word," I said. I was probably making a big deal out of nothing at all. "He didn't say anything. He was there when we went to the wedding, and I thought it odd that he was still there when we came out much later."

"Come to think of it, I don't know him, which is odd in Nivan. We don't see too many strangers around here. I know almost everyone either on a first name basis or at least by sight. I'll have someone check up on him if he's still hanging around tomorrow."

"That would be great." I felt relieved. It seemed unlikely that the Sons of the Heavenly Father would have gone to all the trouble to follow me here, but you never know. If Airik could confirm the stranger was from Koccoran it would make me feel better.

By the time we got into the room, it was all I could do to stumble to the couch.

"Are you intoxicated?" he asked, looking at me with a bemused expression on his face.

"I am really drunk," I said. "You should have warned me about the pink stuff."

"Sorry."

He looked uncomfortable and sat down beside me without touching my body. He had minimized physical contact all night. I was beginning to think I had imagined the heat in his eyes earlier.

"I have to explain something to you, and I hope you're sober enough to understand it."

I hiccupped. "I'm sober enough to understand anything," I said.

"Sure you are," he said, a tiny smile on his face. "What I'm about to tell you might sound archaic, but it is another part of our cultural rules."

"Yes?" I said, trying to look serious but feeling like giggling at his alien culture.

"We're not legally married yet."

"What? But we stood in front of that man, said some words and you gave me these." I held up my hands to show the rings.

"Yes. That's all important. But there's one more thing that is necessary to make the marriage legal."

"What's that?" I said, having absolutely no idea what he meant.

"We have to consummate it," he said, watching me carefully for my reaction.

My eyebrows went up, and my nipples got hard. I felt a flash of lightning race down to my core.

"Consummated." I repeated.

He nodded.

"We can't just tell them we did because they perform tests the morning after. We only get the marriage certificate after our examinations are complete." His eyes were closed, and he had a pained expression on his face.

I stared at him.

"They're going to verify we mated?"

He nodded. I think he expected me to be appalled. On a purely intellectual level, I was a bit scandalized. But on a physical level, my body was doing a happy dance. I was going to get lucky tonight. This was what Neesa meant when she had talked about needing chemistry between Airik and me tonight.

In any event, my intellectual side had to put up token resistance.

"We don't even know each other."

"You never had a one-night stand, Quinn?" he murmured.

"I have," I said, honestly.

"How well did you know him?"

"Good point," I said. I couldn't even remember his name. "But isn't there a clause in the TerraMates contract that says I don't have to sleep with you if I don't want to?"

"Do you honestly find the thought of having sex with me abhorrent?" he asked. His expression showed a worry and vulnerability that made me want to reassure him immediately. "Of course, I would never dream of forcing you," he added before I could say anything.

"Of course not. And I don't find it at all abhorrent. I was dreaming about it this afternoon. You're quite attractive, Airik." I couldn't help the heat that crept up my cheeks. I couldn't let him think I didn't want him.

"You were dreaming about us?" Our eyes connected and held. This time, I couldn't stand to have him so far away from me. I needed a passionate kiss, not the chaste kind he'd been giving me all evening.

I stood up unsteadily and walked over to him.

"Have you heard about the underwear a Koccoran woman wears on her wedding day, Airik?" I said, wrapping my arms around his neck and pressing my breasts up against his chest. I wasn't usually this forward. The pink drink must be making me bold.

"There are rumors. Men aren't allowed to see it. We're not supposed to know about it until our wedding night."

"It's designed to give you access," I said, looking him deep in the eyes.

"To what?" he said, licking his lips.

"To the important parts of my body."

He swallowed, and I watched his Adam's apple bob up and down. I kissed it. He pulled in a deep breath.

"Do you want to help me out of this gown?" I said. "It's tight and constricting."

"It would be my pleasure," he said, leading me over to the bedroom.

Airik took his sweet time stripping me out of my dress. I didn't mind being free. I wasn't thinking thoroughly about my actions while I was drunk. The fact that I wanted him badly helped. But who was I kidding? I had gone home with a stranger from the bar on a night long ago. My husband was next to me. There was nothing wrong with a husband and wife enjoying conjugal relations.

He unbuttoned me slowly, planting kisses all the way down. He periodically stopped for us to make out like teenagers, our tongues twisting around each other. Every time he kissed me, I got more and bothered for him. Once he had me out of the dress, the sexy, naughty underwear made me squirm with need.

He made full use of the underwear to access the vital parts of my anatomy. Finally, we were both naked.

"Quinn, I can't wait anymore."

"Me neither, Airik," I said, panting. "Do you have protection?"

"Protection against what?"

"A condom or something, to make sure I don't get pregnant."

"Why wouldn't you want to get pregnant?"

"Are you kidding me?"

"Right, you didn't get the brochure on Koccoran. The short version of the story is that we have an extremely low birth rate due to environmental conditions. There's no such thing as birth control here. It's against the law to prevent conception."

"We get to do it with nothing between us?" I said.

"What other way is there?"

"Well, we have these things called condoms on Earth. They're like a latex glove that wraps around your..."

He made a disgusted face.

"Yeah, it's not as much fun. I mean, I've never done it without a condom. But I imagine it feels better with nothing between us." I felt myself tingling at the thought of his flesh against mine.

"Airik, I need you inside me, right now," I said, pressing my hips up towards his hardness.

"Quinn," he breathed, and I felt him at my entrance.

"Yes, yes, please, Airik."

I felt like a wanton, but it had been a long time for me. I needed this. He pushed inside. I gasped at the size of him. I hadn't got a good look, but he was quite the handful.

"You're tight, Quinn," he said.

"It's been a while," I told him, panting as he pressed in further. "And I've only done it a handful of times."

"I'm not complaining," he said as he thrust in more.

I felt myself opening for him. My inner muscles stretched to accommodate him. "Jesus, that feels good," I said.

He bent and sucked one of my nipples into his mouth, scoring it with his teeth. It made my hips jerk, plunging him deeper inside me.

I was breathing quickly. I cried out as he drove in hard, embedding himself completely inside me.

"Oh, fuck, Airik."

He kissed me passionately. I squirmed beneath him. Our bodies were slick with sweat. Then he began thrusting rhythmically in and out, touching a bundle of nerves I hadn't noticed in the past.

I didn't know what he was doing, but I knew I was enjoying it more than I ever had before. Soon I felt my pleasure rise. Heat started pouring from my core into every corner of my body. I didn't know that when women said they were hot for a man, they meant physical temperature.

Every time our pelvises hit together, he rubbed against my clit and another spot inside me. He had his head bent, sucking my breasts. My desire ratcheted up several notches, and I moaned, unable to stop myself. I had never felt like this before. Airik began whispering to me in an alien language. I didn't understand what he was saying, but it sounded sexy. I thought I would come right then.

"Faster, please, Airik," I said.

He increased his speed, driving into me and making me crazy.

"Oh, yes. Yes, that feels so good," I said.

I felt the intensity rising higher and higher until it peaked. I exploded with the longest, hottest orgasm of my life. I screamed and writhed as I convulsed around him.

"I'm going to come," he said. Then he stiffened and groaned. I felt his seed filling me. It made the spasms increase again as if my body wanted to pull every drop out of him.

Finally, we lay still, with him on top of me and still inside.

When he rolled off of me, I let out a little sound of dismay when I felt us separate. He pulled me close to him. My back was against his chest, and I smiled.

"That was unbelievable," he said in my ear.

"I have never, ever experienced anything like that in my life before," I told him truthfully.

"Me neither, Quinn," he said. I felt him smiling into my shoulder. "It's an auspicious beginning, I think."

"Very auspicious," I said, rolling a little so I could kiss him.

Our lips felt like they had been made to kiss each other and soon we were lost again. This was going to be a long night.

I was confident we would pass the test.

CHAPTER 7

QUINN

We received our marriage certificates after we got tested. We each gave a swab of our saliva for DNA testing that proved our identities. A machine spit out a rectangular sticker.

The man processing our marriage certificates smoothed the label on my left arm. Right arms were for birth certificates. After a minute, when I moved my arm back and forth, I could see our marriage information. The date of the wedding, our names, and a photo of Airik and me.

Once he did the same steps on Airik, we were legally married. We got dressed to go outside again. Airik took my hand as we walked out of the building and back into the bitter cold. Even though I had three layers on and wore more clothing than him, I still felt chilled.

"We're only getting two days of honeymoon," he said. "I'm not taking off of work."

Because this wasn't a real marriage, I thought.

"Where do you work?"

"I'm a senior admin for the government. I don't want to talk about work right now. I'm already a bit of a workaholic, and this is supposed to be our honeymoon."

"Of course. That's fine. We have all year to get to know each other," I said. I didn't care. I was on a high today.

"I was wondering something," he said. He opened the door for me to a small snow car waiting outside the building.

"Is this one self-driving?"

"Yes. I own this one. They don't all have drivers. The ones in town are self-driving. Any cars that go out of town need drivers because the terrain or the snow can require human intervention. That brings me back to what I was wondering," he said. The look in his eyes gave me shivers. "Is it possible you're wearing your special underwear like I asked you to?"

I smiled at him, feeling as sexy as I ever had in my life.

"Maybe I am."

"I was hoping you'd say that."

"You mean I didn't wear this skirt for nothing?" I said, indicating my attire. "I wanted to make sure you had access if you needed it."

He didn't say anything as his hand slipped under my skirt. He sucked in his breath when he discovered how much access he had to me. He set the car to the slowest speed possible on the way home.

I saw him again. It was when we stepped into the hotel and pulled off our mitts and hats. The man from yesterday disappeared down one of the halls.

"Did you see him again, Airik?" I asked, feeling a spike of fear pierce my heart. He might be randomly staying at the hotel, but my intuition told me otherwise. I had learned a long time ago that it was always right. "Will you have him checked out? You don't think I'm crazy, right?"

I wished again that my Dad was here. He had always been my protector. But he wasn't here, and I would have to get used to it, despite my heartache for him and anything familiar from home.

"Sure, Quinn. But why are you worried? I think you had better tell me."

Tell him? I couldn't tell him the whole story, but I would have to give him something.

"It sounds silly, but when I left home, I was being persecuted. There was a cult that was trying to...well, they were attempting to kill me. I'm afraid they might have followed me here."

"Pursuing you seems unlikely when you consider the expense," Airik said.

"I'm probably just being paranoid." I tried to dismiss my concern just like he did.

"I'll check him out if you want, Quinn. I'll send you the information."

"Thanks, Airik. I appreciate it," I said, smiling up at my new husband. Maybe I had imagined things after all.

I had the vision after we made love again in the hotel room. It took me when we were snuggling in bed. As usual, I was sucked into a movie that was playing in my mind. But it wasn't a movie. It was the future.

I felt my body go rigid and start to shake. I stared into space, not seeing what was in front of me. I was walking down the street holding a little hand. I looked down and saw a two-year-old girl. We were walking down the street near the building where I received the marriage certificate. There was no snow around me, so it must be summer.

I went to cross the street. We were in the middle when the little girl dropped her doll. There was a car coming towards us. I pulled her across the street to save her. At the last moment, she yanked her hand away from me and ran back for the doll. She grabbed it and picked it up, beaming at me. She didn't see the car when it hit, and her body went flying through the air. I didn't need to touch her body to know she was gone. She was lying still without any movement. I screamed and ran to her, dropping down beside the lifeless little body as I started to sob.

As I came out of the vision, I saw Airik staring at me. "Quinn? Thank goodness you're back."

"Airik?"

"Are you all right? What happened?"

My eyes filled with tears. I knew I wouldn't be able to sleep tonight. If I did, nightmares of the girl's death would torment me.

I looked up at him. He appeared concerned. "It seemed as though you were having a seizure," he said.

He had a great explanation for me, and it wasn't even much of a lie.

"This kind of thing used to happen to me back home," I said. "I'm sorry. I should have told you, so you wouldn't worry when it happened." It was all true.

"I was worried."

I reached up and touched his face. "You don't have to be. I'm all right."

"You look upset," he said, tracing a line the tear had made down my face.

"I always feel a little strange afterward," I said, dropping my eyes. "I need to rest."

"Okay," he said. "I'll find something to occupy myself."

I nodded. "I'll rest here."

Once I was sure he was gone, I broke down and cried.

AIRIK

We had just made love again when it happened. Her body went stiff, and she started shaking. Her eyes became unfocused. She stared off into space. I watched in consternation.

What was going on?

Different intense emotions passed across her face. Happiness. Careful attention. Worry. Anger. Terror. Grief.

Without warning, she was back. Her shaking stopped, and she looked up at me, telling me this had happened before, and it was nothing.

I let her give me a story about a seizure. When I went into the other room, I couldn't concentrate.

I knew Quinn was lying to me.

Along with my ability to receive Precogs about the future, I was also an empath. I could feel people's emotions. The emotion I sensed from Quinn right now was guilt.

But why would she lie about having seizures? There was nothing shameful about them at all. Her behavior was strange. Something different was going on. I needed to find out what she was hiding. I had linked my life with this woman without knowing anything about her. Right now, I thought that had been a bad idea.

I needed to find out the truth. If I couldn't trust Quinn, then this was never going to work.

QUINN

It was three o'clock in the morning. I still couldn't sleep. I had watched three movies and tried every trick I knew to get myself to fall asleep.

As soon as I closed my eyes, I would see the little girl dead and broken on the ground.

I made myself so sick from crying that my stomach hurt.

Airik, of course, was sleeping like a log in the other room.

I got into my messages and saw one from Airik about the stranger and also one from my father. I opened my Dad's message first. I needed something to cheer me up.

When I started reading, I wished I hadn't opened it. It wasn't good news. Dad said he had recently watched a news program about the Sons of the Heavenly Father. The police had captured several members. Two had told the police everything they knew. Former cult members said the organization had people all over the galaxy and on every planet. Cult members were encouraged to seek out and kill anyone who seemed different.

They were fanatical, he said. The cult's lone assassins would go to great extremes to kill someone who had been targeted previously as a victim. He encouraged me to be vigilant and careful in my new home. Maybe I wasn't as safe as we had hoped. He also sent me congratulations on my wedding. Tears ran down my face by the time I finished his message, but I still managed to open the one from Airik.

Airik's message was a copy and paste. All the man's profile information was in front of me. I wondered if Airik had read it. I thought it unlikely. The message didn't have any personal greetings, and he hadn't seemed concerned when I told him about my worries.

I scanned the information. The man was human. Was on a work visa on Koccoran. Wasn't married. Had graduated from high school but not college. I scrolled down looking for the pertinent information I needed. Religious affiliations. Where was it?

There. Near the end. Religious affiliations: **a member of the Sons of the Heavenly Father church**

I jumped up and began to pace. Suddenly, the fear for my life eclipsed my grief at seeing the little girl die. If I were back home, I would go for a run. But here with three feet of snow outside, it was impossible. I felt trapped and frustrated. Sometimes exercise helped when I felt isolated like this, but I couldn't go out.

It wouldn't be safe to go out, either.

I supposed I could do some exercises inside. I started with some jumping jacks, then proceeded to sit-ups, push-ups, running on the spot, and burpies. I dripped with sweat and felt exhausted. I sat on the floor with my arms wrapped around my knees.

I was exhausted, but not sleepy.

I decided to take a shower. As I got up, Airik came out of the room, rubbing his eyes. "Quinn? Are you still awake?"

"Yeah, I can't sleep. It's no big deal; it happens all the time. Don't worry. You'll get used to it. I hope I didn't wake you."

"Uh, no. I didn't hear you." He looked uncertain, which I found perplexing. Either I had woken him, or I hadn't. "But why can't you sleep? Is something wrong?"

He was giving me a penetrating stare and his eyes looked wide awake. He was making me nervous all of a sudden. Did he suspect I was psychic and that I had visions? What would have made him think that? I didn't know what I did while having a vision, but my dad said I never spoke.

What would have tipped him off?

"Nothing's wrong. I have nightmares sometimes and can't go back to sleep." This was true, though not the entire truth. I would decide what to tell him about the man from the lobby in the morning after I had a few hours of sleep under my belt.

"Really? Me too, sometimes."

I didn't believe him. "I was exercising to try and make myself tired. I'm going to have a shower."

"Let me use the bathroom first."

"Sure," I said, gesturing for him to proceed.

It was an incredibly awkward conversation. I wondered how we went so quickly from being as close as two people can be to barely being able to make small talk. I shook my head. Maybe I shouldn't be hiding things from him. He was my husband. Surely he would understand, right?

Of course not. No one ever understood. I was a freak, an outcast, and a weirdo. He wouldn't get it. No one would ever get me.

That's the way my life was.

He came back out of the bathroom.

"How about something different? Quinn, you said you've never seen snow before, right? Have you ever heard of rainbow snow?"

"What's that?"

"It's a weather phenomenon that creates a swirling light effect that looks like colored snow. It looks spectacular. I checked, and the observation point will be open tomorrow. They're expecting a rainbow swirl. Would you like to go?

"Sure," I said, smiling at him. He walked over to me and pulled me in for a soft kiss. When our lips touched, I felt like there was nothing between us. When he let me go, I felt the distance growing between us again.

"I hope you'll come back to bed," he said, studying me.

I shrugged. I felt far away from him, and I didn't like it.

"I probably won't unless I think I can sleep. Otherwise, I'll toss and turn and wake you up."

"Okay then," he said, looking at me like he didn't believe a word I said. With a sad glance, he went back into the bedroom.

I sat down on the couch then and hung my head. If Airik couldn't trust me, I knew this marriage couldn't last.

AIRIK

We stood at the top of the hill and looked down. There was snow everywhere and from up here we had an excellent view. Before us, the town spread out — the colored buildings stood out brightly against the white of the snow on the streets. Some of the houses had smoke coming from their chimneys. All around the town was the forest, looking like a thick green carpet from our viewpoint.

We were waiting in line for our turn to get on one of the open hovercraft. It would take us to the proper height so we could see the beautiful rainbow swirls.

The weather was perfect. I was sure Quinn was going to like it. I looked over at her and checked to make sure the scarf covered her delicate cheeks. The only visible part of her was her bright blue eyes, the color of the sky today.

"Warm enough?" I said with a smile.

She was wearing panties, long underwear, and two pairs of pants, not including her snow pants. On top, she had on her bra, a camisole, a long underwear shirt, a sweater and her coat. She had on warm boots and a hat on her head, with a scarf wrapped around her face. I knew all this because I had enjoyed watching her dress before we left. I hoped she was warm enough. There was no way she could carry any more clothes on her tiny frame.

She pulled down the scarf and grinned at me.

"I am. I'm glad I put on everything. For once, I'm not freezing."

"We're going to have to toughen you up and get you outside more. There's still three more months of the first winter."

"Three?" she winced.

"Winter is lots of fun," I said as we moved forward in line. "When we get on the hovercraft, you'll see the beauty of your new home. It wouldn't be possible without the cold weather."

"I hope so," she said, tilting her head to look up at the vehicles already floating in the sky. Soon it was our turn. We strapped on the seat belts.

"Are you ready?" I said, peeking my head around so I could see her. She turned and kissed me. Then she smiled, looking happy but nervous.

"Ready."

The hovercraft began rising into the air, avoiding the other vehicles and taking us to the best view of the snow. When the hovercraft stopped, I heard Quinn draw in a deep breath.

"Airik, I've never seen anything as lovely as this."

Rainbow snow was only visible at certain times of the year. The primary component of snowflakes here was clear ice. It looked like they were constructed from glass.

The snowflakes split the sunlight like small prisms. The wind created a swirling rainbow vortex that moved and danced in the sky.

We sat there for a long time watching it. Quinn took my hand in hers, and we didn't say anything. Finally, she said she was cold. I directed the hovercraft to descend.

"That was incredible," she said, kissing me on the cheek once we were on solid ground again. "I've never seen anything like it."

"Do you want to go downtown and get a snack?" I asked. I didn't want this day to end yet. I took her to a cafe I liked. We had warm drinks and a delicious Koccoran bread filled with spices and dried fruit.

When we got back to the hotel, we took off all our outdoor clothes and hung them around the room. There was a drying rack in our room for our mitts. After we had changed into our pajamas, I went into the kitchen.

"Do you want some tea, Quinn?" I called out.

"Sure."

When I turned around, she was behind me. She smiled and wrapped her arms around my waist.

"Thank you for a wonderful day. Rainbow snow is the most beautiful thing I have ever seen."

"I'm glad you enjoyed it. I haven't been up to see rainbow snow in years. I had a good time, too."

I leaned down and pressed a kiss to her forehead on the spot between her eyebrows directly on her third eye. I didn't mean to kiss her there. It just happened to be within easy reach as I bent down.

As I touched her third eye, the cortex of all intuition and precognition, images rushed through my mind. I used my training to slow them down.

Quinn as a little girl, happy and carefree, with a man who must be her father, pushing her on a swing. Quinn riding a bike. Quinn wearing a fancy dress and dancing at a party. A teenage Quinn, unhappy now, crying on her father's shoulder. Quinn sitting on the same couch with her face beaten up. Quinn hiding in an apartment.

As my lips came away, the flow of images stopped, and Quinn looked up at me with shock in her eyes.

"What is it?" I whispered. I wanted to understand.

I was a top recruiter for the Precog Division before I was a director. One of the ways to identify a Precog was by touching their third eye using skin-to-skin contact. It allowed a trained Precog to sense their abilities. I had been one of the best.

Quinn must be a Precog. There was no other explanation.

She stepped away from me and she started babbling.

"It was nothing, Airik. Nothing at all."

"That wasn't nothing."

"It was. I swear. Please. Just ignore it." She looked around the room like she wanted to escape.

"Quinn," I said, using my most authoritative voice. "There's something you're not telling me. I have to know what it is."

CHAPTER 8

QUINN

My heart pounded, my stomach churned, and I couldn't seem to get enough air. I was panicking. The scar on my neck always bothered me in stressful situations. It was aching right now. I rubbed it, trying to ease the pain. I couldn't meet Airik's eyes. He spoke in a commanding voice.

"Quinn. There's something you're not telling me. I want to know what it is."

I had to get out of here. I know I wasn't thinking clearly, but I wanted to get away from him. I couldn't tell him my secret. Bad things always happened when people found out I'm a psychic. Someone was about to make fun of me, bully me, bothered me, or beat me up.

He was waiting.

The last things I saw before I bolted and ran for the door were his beautiful brown eyes.

"Quinn!" he shouted.

I had left already. I've always been a good runner. I was on the track team every year in high school. And I won. When I was scared, I was even faster.

I raced down the hall and jumped onto the stairs, skittering and sliding down the steps. I only saved myself from tumbling head over heels because I was holding on to the railing.

I heard Airik enter the stairwell. He was shouting my name and saying things in a language I didn't understand, but I guess cursing sounds the same on all the planets.

When I reached the ground floor, I ran straight into the lobby and out the door, forgetting about the weather conditions. Fortunately, there was a car waiting outside the door for a passenger. I jumped in and requested a random destination. I could change it later. I didn't think about where I was going or what I was doing.

I needed to get away.

The car pulled away from the curb and took off down the street. I turned around to look back when it was making a turn and saw Airik standing outside the hotel, looking back and forth down the street.

Maybe I was wrong. I had been so panicked that I ran without thinking about what I was doing. But now that I was away from the situation and calming down, I realized that I had severely overreacted. Maybe he meant something else. Even if he didn't, he was my husband, and Airik had a right to know what sort of woman he had married.

I let the vehicle wander the streets for over two hours before I told it to return to the hotel. I felt like an idiot. I didn't want to go back and apologize, but what was I going to do? We were married, like it or not, for the next year. I had no money to return to Earth. It would be foolish and dangerous, even if I could.

I swiped my ID over the payment machine and hopped out, sprinting back inside. I shivered; I should have grabbed a jacket, at least.

It occurred to me that he must need to be married for his reasons, too. He probably wouldn't want to escape our marriage.

Maybe he would when he found out about me.

For once, as I climbed the stairs back up to our floor, I wanted to tell someone about my visions. I wanted to get everything off my chest. I was tired of hiding part of myself. I could only hope he understood and didn't send me packing the moment I told him. If everything went well, he wouldn't hate me too much.

I walked up to our door and hesitated. My hand was poised to knock. I tried to work up my courage when the door flew open, and I saw Airik. He grabbed my hand and pulled me into the room.

"Quinn! Thank goodness you're all right," he said, enfolding me in his arms. I blinked, completely taken by surprise. He had been anxious about me. "I was worried you would get lost, or that your terrible friend would be bothering you. You didn't even take your cold weather clothes, so I thought you might freeze to death. You know that you can die from the cold, right?"

"Airik," I said, trying to slow him down. "I'm okay. I rode around in a car the whole time. It might be pretty expensive."

He shrugged.

"I don't care. But why did you run out? What were you so scared of?"

"What?" I said, wondering what he thought it was.

"Was it me?" He looked agonized at the thought that I might fear him.

"No," I said, shaking my head. "No. It's not that at all."

"But you don't want to tell me about it?" He seemed to be hurt. I regretted not telling him before now.

"It's not that I don't want to tell you," I said, gazing up at him. He was very handsome, but I needed to focus. "I'm worried about how you'll take what I have to say."

"It can't be that bad, can it?" Now he looked apprehensive.

"I don't know," I said, dropping my eyes. "When people find out, they usually do bad things to me."

"Like teasing you and beating you up?" he said, his eyes full of compassion.

"Yes," I said. "How did you know?"

"Just tell me, Quinn," he whispered. He put his hands on my cheeks and kissed me on the forehead in the same spot as before. Visions flashed through my head.

I could understand the visions now, not like the first two times he kissed my forehead. They had gone by too quickly for me to see them before.

The visions were of Airik. *Airik as a baby, riding on his father's shoulders. Airik being rocked in his mother's arms. Airik sliding. Airik swimming with his brothers and sisters. Then teenage Airik sitting still in a room all by himself with his eyes closed. Airik receiving a diploma. Airik reading a letter that said he had his dream job. Airik saving a young man's life.*

As he pulled away from me, he said it again.

"Tell me what you saw, Quinn."

"How do you know I saw anything?"

He waited patiently.

I swallowed and sat down on the couch. He came and sat beside me, taking my hand.

Every instinct in my body told me to hide it from him just like I had hidden it from everyone else, all my life. I didn't listen.

"I have visions," I said.

And he smiled. He looked relieved. Vindicated, even. He nodded. "Go on."

His reaction was peculiar, but I didn't let it stop me from telling my story. "They started when I was fourteen. I've had them off and on ever since. My father and I tried everything we could to get rid of them, but nothing worked. I try to ignore them now. They won't stop coming."

I glanced over at him. He wasn't getting out any matches yet.

"After we made love, when I told you I was having a seizure?" He nodded. "I had a vision."

"And then you couldn't sleep," he said. It seemed like everything was making sense to him.

"It's hard to relax when I see someone die, and I know I can't do anything about it." I said. My voice grew softer and softer. "Especially when it's a child."

I felt grief overwhelm me again. Tears begin spilling out of my eyes. It wasn't just because I felt the emotion of losing the child. I also felt the relief of finally telling someone what was happening to me without judgment. When I dared to look at him again, he was staring at me with such compassion and kindness that I actually started to cry.

He didn't tell me not to cry. He just held me. It was the most comforting thing anyone had ever done for me. When I finally stopped crying, after I had blown my nose and wiped my eyes, I looked up at him.

"Do you want to send me back now?" I said in a small voice.

He laughed then. I didn't know how he could be so jolly when I had just told him a deep, dark secret.

"I don't think sending you back is an option. I wouldn't want to, even if I could."

"Why not? Don't you hate me or think I'm a witch? Maybe you're thinking about burning me at the stake."

The smile left his face. "You're serious."

I nodded, avoiding his eyes. That's why he wasn't upset. He thought I was joking.

"People treated you that way, Quinn? Because of your gift?"

I made a face. "Sometimes it feels more like a curse."

"It's a gift." He put his hand under my chin, forcing me to look at him.

"Not where I come from," I said, tears in my eyes again.

"Well," he said, smiling broadly. "I guess you're lucky you're here."

"What are you talking about, Airik?" I stared at him in bewilderment.

"It's too bad you didn't read the folder on Koccoran, Quinn. You could have saved yourself a lot of worry."

"Why?" I frowned.

"Because," he said, smiling broadly at me. "You happen to have landed yourself on a planet full of psychics."

I felt my mouth drop open. I knew I was staring, but I couldn't help it.

"You've got to be kidding me."

"It's no lie, Quinn. You'll fit right in around here."

I wrapped my arms around him, and he hugged me tightly. I couldn't keep tears from leaking out. I pulled away from him quickly, hungry for more information.

"Tell me everything."

He grinned and pulled out a computer. He quickly retrieved official-looking documents with the Koccoran government logo.

"This describes the Precog Division of the government," he said, glancing sideways at me. "It's my division. I'm the Director."

"Of the whole division?"

"Yep. I'm the youngest ever to hold the post. It was a great honor to get it. I've been working my whole life towards this position. That's why I needed to marry you, in fact. To keep my job."

"I wondered what it was."

105

"My career is everything to me, Quinn. I would do anything to keep it, even marry a stranger."

"Why would you have to get married to keep your job?"

"We have a requirement called The Akuna. You have to be married by a certain age, or else there are consequences. If you ask me, it's an old law and should be abolished."

"Wow," I said, stunned by his revelation. Something else dawned on me.

"Precog? As in precognition? Like Precogs who have visions?"

He nodded.

"So I'm a Precog?" I asked, trying to wrap my head around the sudden shift in perspective. On Earth, I had to conceal my abilities. On this planet, they were desired.

"I believe you are."

"If that's your division, does that make you a Precog too? You're like me?"

"I have visions too. I'm in charge of all the Precogs. What is it, Quinn?" He was staring into my eyes with such compassion that I almost broke down.

"I've never met anyone who was like me," I said. I felt joyful as he looked solemn.

"I'm sorry for the way you've been treated in the past, Quinn. I hope you will come to see your power as a gift here on Koccoran." He smiled, looking deeply into my eyes that were bright with tears.

"Maybe," I said, shrugging.

"How about we order some food and talk about it more over dinner? We'll make it a date."

I smiled. "A date? With my husband? Who's a Precog?" I pulled him in for a kiss. "That sounds perfect."

AIRIK

I sat across the table from Quinn. It was hard for me to stop gazing into her fascinating blue eyes. I thought for a moment about what she had been through because of her gift, and it made me sad. It was such a waste of talent.

Quinn started eating her food. "Okay, spill," she said. "What does a division full of people who see visions of the future do? It's not like we can change things. Do you record everything for posterity? That way, the newspapers can have their stories and obituaries ready a few days ahead of time?"

She was joking. I smiled uncomfortably. She had many misconceptions that needed clarification. I didn't know where to start. Maybe I should knock out the biggest one first.

"Quinn, listen to me. I don't know what happened to you in the past. You need to clear your mind of everything you thought you knew about your gift."

She stared at me as she chewed.

"The future can be changed, Quinn. That's what my division does. We have visions. Many of them are about death. We are trained to open more to those insights to find out when a person is going to die. Then we can go in and save them."

"All of them?"

"Almost all of them, unless something goes wrong with the intervention. We have an underpopulation problem on Koccoran. We want as many people as possible to die a natural death. Most people do."

"Why is the birth rate so low?" she said curiously.

"I'm not sure. It's something about the environment, and it's been a problem for as long as I can remember. There have always been people who could have visions and who had other mental abilities. My ancestors soon figured out how to use their images to save people's lives. Since then, the problem with the low birth rate has been balanced out with the number of people we save from early death."

"You sound like a bunch of superheroes," she said admiringly. She took a bite, chewed, and swallowed.

"I don't know what that means, but I'll take it as a compliment."

"I meant it as one," she said. "How does your division operate?"

"Here's how it works." I started recited a workflow that was familiar to me, but foreign to her. It was fascinating to see things through her eyes.

"A Precog has a vision and alerts their Recorder. We have partners who help us write down visions as they're happening."

"You can do other things while you're having a vision?"

"We've had thousands of years to improve our mental abilities, Quinn. We have it down to a science. In fact, it *is* science. Did you wonder why you had flashes of images when I kissed you? I touched a particular part of your brain that controls intuition and precognition."

"I didn't know there was such a thing."

"I used to be a Recruiter before I became Director. Recruiters are always on the hunt for more Precogs. The easiest way to tell if someone's a Precog is to touch the spot on their intuition and precognition cortex."

"You kissed all your recruits?" she said. She had a funny look on her face.

"No," I said, laughing and taking a sip of my drink. "I would put my hand on their third eye. It has to be skin to skin contact. I touched your third eye by accident."

"What happens after the recording?"

"The visions are analyzed and cross-referenced. Often several Precogs will have visions of the same event. Once we get a few different versions of the same story, we have a good idea of what's going to happen."

"Okay."

"Then we pass the information to the ground team. If there's a preventable death, they're responsible for going out and saving lives."

"That sounds incredible. I tried to prevent one death that I foresaw. It turned out badly for me."

"Well, we can't save everyone but we do manage to prevent many deaths."

"I can't believe it."

"It's my life."

She stared at me. "You're a lucky guy. I've never even had a job. I spent years hiding my gift."

"I think that should change, starting immediately."

"How?"

"We can always use more talented Precogs. I think you should apply for training."

"Are you saying I could work as a Precog in your division?" The idea hadn't occurred to her.

"What do you think?" I asked, smoothing her hair away from her forehead.

"It sounds like heaven."

"A job at the Division is work. But this?" I leaned down and kissed her deeply. When we came up for air a few minutes later, I grinned at her. "This *is* heaven."

Quinn was, quite frankly, an amazing woman. She was intelligent, beautiful, sexy, and a talented Precog from what I could see, especially since no one had ever trained her. I wasn't in love with her, but I was pretty impressed by my wife.

It broke my heart that she had been treated horribly for having a gift like precognition. That's how it was on some of the backwater planets. I was lucky to be born here on Koccoran. I wondered again what her planet of origin was. Kartar hadn't given me any details. But I reminded myself that I didn't really want to know.

To me, she was just Quinn. I would find out about her as we went along. Right now, she was folding her clothes and packing them in an overnight bag to move into my apartment.

"I was thinking," I said. "Maybe I shouldn't go to work today. We could go apartment hunting instead."

"I thought you had a place."

"I do," I said. Explaining myself was embarrassing. "Now that we're married, I feel like we should start fresh and have something new together." *In a place where every room doesn't remind me of Sornalee.*

I wondered if she would think my idea was stupid. I ignored a tiny tab of guilt that I was betraying my true love by striving for happiness with Quinn. But I reminded myself that I had committed to this year. I was going to do it properly. What happened after our divorce would be a different story.

"Are you sure you want to do that?" She stopped folding, forgetting the shirt in her lap.

"I do, Quinn. I want this to work. I like you, and we have chemistry. I want us to be happy together."

"Well then," she said, her eyes shining. "When do we start?"

"What do you think of this one?" I asked. I turned in the space of the living room and caught a faint scent of fish.

Quinn wrinkled her delicate nose and shrugged.

"No? I have one more on my list. The realtor is supposed to meet us there in twenty minutes."

"Okay," she said, but she didn't look hopeful the way she had at the beginning of the day.

When we got there, her eyes lit up immediately, and we smiled at each other. It was perfect. I had known it before we walked in. As we followed the realtor on the tour, I held Quinn's hand. I kept getting flashes of us in this place in the future.

Quinn making supper at the counter in the kitchen. Me working in the office. Us curled up on the couch watching a movie. Quinn having a vision on the floor in the bathroom. Me carrying her over my shoulder to the bedroom. Us making love on the table in the dining room.

I glanced at Quinn. Her face was a delicate pink color again. I wondered if she was getting the visions at the same time I was.

I thanked the realtor and asked if we could have a few moments in private to discuss the place. When he shut the door, I turned to Quinn.

"Well?"

"I love it. And you do too, don't you? I can tell now."

"I do. I think it's perfect."

"Well, and there's the possibilities." She trailed off, biting her lip and dropping her gaze.

"The visions?" I waggled my eyebrows, and she grinned.

"The last one was intense."

"Yes, it was," I said.

"Does that mean we're going to live here? Are all those things going to happen?"

"That's usually what it means. But what specifically did you see?"

She listed off all the things I had seen in my mind, blushing bright red again when she told me about making love on the dining room table.

"Rooms must be christened, after all," I said.

She laughed, putting her hand to her crimson face.

I stopped short all of a sudden as I came to a realization.

"What is it, Airik?" she said, studying me.

"Did you have those visions as we were walking through the rooms?"

She nodded.

"It almost seems as if we had them simultaneously. That's unusual to say the least. I've never heard of people having simultaneous visions before."

"What does it mean?"

"I don't know, Quinn. I don't know." I gazed at her a moment longer before pushing the thoughts aside and changing the subject back to the apartment.

"Are we taking this place?"

She nodded happily.

"Sweet. I'll have someone clean it, and we can stay here tonight."

"Tonight?"

"Why not? It will be like camping. I'll take care of all the paperwork. Watch for a message from me to sign it. I'm putting it in both of our names." I started walking out the door. I was going to let the realtor know of our decision but stopped when I saw the look on her face. She looked surprised and gratified that both our names would be on the lease.

"We're married, Quinn."

"I know. But I don't know what that means."

I walked over and put my hands on her shoulders. "I don't know exactly either. To me, it means that we're partners. Equal partners. Lovers. Friends. Who knows what the future will bring?"

She nodded.

"Okay. Partners, lovers, friends, and...who knows."

"That's right. Watch for my message."

"I'll catch a car back to the hotel and get the rest of my stuff packed up."

After I had talked to the realtor, we went outside together. When I glanced at her, she was frowning.

"What is it?" I asked.

"It's just..." She glanced at me and changed what she was going to say, smiling falsely. I could tell something was wrong. "It's nothing."

"Tell me," I said insistently.

"It's just that I thought I saw that guy from the hotel again. I don't know if you read your research report, but he's a member of the Sons of the Heavenly Father."

" Why didn't you tell me before? They're the ones who tried to kidnap you, right?"

She nodded.

"And he's on my planet following you around?"

"It seems that way," she said. Her face looked calm, but I could sense fear coming off her in waves.

"You need to be careful. I'm going to alert the police about him. You shouldn't go out without me, okay?"

"Okay," she said in a small voice.

"Don't worry. The police will apprehend him. If he even so much as looked the wrong way when he crossed the street, and it's on his record, they'll have him deported." I kissed her and held her face in my hands. "As your husband, it's my job to keep you safe, Quinn. And I'm going to do it."

She didn't look reassured.

We took a car together back to the hotel. I made sure she was safe in the room before heading back out to find someone to clean our new apartment...and install a security system.

That night, Quinn and I sat on the floor against the wall, the remains of our meal beside us.

"Do you really think I should apply to the Training Institute?" Quinn said, glancing up at me.

I picked up my glass of wine and took a drink. "If I were still a Recruiter, I would be advising you to apply as soon as possible."

"I've never done anything like this before. Having my ability out in the open like that for everyone to see makes me uncomfortable, Airik."

"I know. But that's thinking from your past life. You have to let it go. It's different here."

She closed her eyes and took a deep breath. "You're right. I'm going to have a new life here. It's what I wanted. It's more than what I wanted. I think I should apply too."

"That's awesome," I said, passing her a computer that sat beside me. She took it, puzzled.

"What do you want me to do with this?"

"Turn it on to start."

It opened to the application I was using to learn English.

"We'll close this," I said, swiping it away.

She looked at me strangely. I didn't want her to ask me about my English lessons. My accent was too terrible right now to show anyone. Maybe in a few months, when I knew more and my accent improved.

I brought up the application for the Training Institute.

"I didn't mean immediately. Do you want me to apply right now?"

"There's no time like the present," I said. "It won't take long. I can help you with any parts you don't understand."

She looked worried. "Airik, if I do this, I need to do it on my own. Not because you're a bigwig in the Precog Division."

"I know. I'm not going to interfere. I can just make the process easier for you."

She looked down at the computer, then back up to me. "Okay, then."

We filled out the application, and she submitted it. Then she turned off the computer and handed it back to me.

"Phew," she said. "I can't believe it was that easy."

"You did it." I smiled.

"Yup. No turning back now."

"Would you want to?"

"Not yet. I'll let you know after I get rejected."

"Now you're being silly," I said, leaning in to kiss her. "Koccoran needs your visions."

She giggled into my lips, which made me want her more. Soon we got carried away again. When we finished and lay on the floor side by side, I gave a sigh of contentment.

"This room's christened, I suppose. Only six more to go."

She laughed out loud and slapped my shoulder.

I remembered my time with Sornalee and couldn't believe I had spent a year and a half with her. That had been forgettable.

This was how a relationship was supposed to be.

QUINN

My life had changed a lot in only a few days. Not long ago, I hid in my father's apartment. I only ventured out on errands in the evenings when I would not be conspicuous. I felt like I was a prisoner in jail and forced to hide who I was.

I still missed my dad terribly, but it wasn't as bad as it was at the beginning. My life here on Koccoran was good, mostly because of Airik.

He was a Precog just like me. The thought still blew me away. Some considered my abilities a gift here. I could change the future. If I did well in my training, I might be one of the ones that saved people from an early, unnecessary death.

Me. A savior.

After all the years of dying inside every time I knew I couldn't save anyone, I would have the opportunity to help the people in my visions. It filled me with hope and happiness. I couldn't wait to get started once I got accepted into the training program.

Airik said that they took everyone in initially. There were evaluations during the first week to decide who would continue. I was nervous having Airik so involved in the application process, but he couldn't help it. A lot of husband and wife teams worked together. I hoped it would be okay.

I felt anxious, and I went to get the mail, just to have something to do. I went down a hall and took an elevator to the lobby. I went into a small room that had the mailboxes, unlocking ours, removing the envelopes and relocking the box. When I turned around to go out, the man from the Sons of the Heavenly Father blocked the doorway.

My heart started to pound. I looked around frantically for a way out, but there was no escape. "Leave me alone," I said.

He grinned. I noticed that he had a tooth missing in the front.

"I don't think so, witch," he said. He wasn't moving towards me, but he wasn't leaving either.

"I'm not a witch. I'm just an ordinary person. Haven't you noticed many people here can do the same things I do?"

"I've noticed, all right. A planet full of freaks," he said, then spat on the floor. I looked at the gob of spittle in disgust.

"What do you want?" I asked, needing to get something out of this guy. Maybe if I kept him talking, he would start to see me as a person.

"I want to see you burn," he said. "Once you're dead, I can get off this alien planet and go back home."

Maybe not. I needed to start bluffing. Maybe I could extract some useful information from him. I wondered if he was working alone and if he would be stupid enough to tell me. It was worth a shot to see what I could find out.

"Where's your partner? You don't think you can take me down by yourself, do you? Didn't you hear about the last guys that attacked me?"

He shuffled nervously. His eyes shifted back and forth.

"We work alone." He seemed to be telling the truth. I was hardly trained in lie detection, so I didn't know if I should believe him.

"The ones who attacked me before weren't working alone," I pointed out.

"They weren't assassins," he said. I noticed he was trying to move his hands together. When he did, he crossed his fingers. I remembered the people who had egged me earlier had done the same thing. Maybe they thought making a cross with their fingers would protect them from me.

"Do you think that you can do something to me?" I said incredulously, trying to look more confident than I felt.

He took a step back. These guys were frightened of me! That's when I realized that I held all the power. I lifted my hands.

"Don't," he said. He looked terrified.

123

I took a step toward him, and he turned and ran. I followed him and watched as he jumped into a car and escaped.

That's when I knew that I had changed since I got here. The old me would have allowed herself to be bullied. I walked back upstairs feeling better than I had in a long time.

Airik came home from work at five o'clock. We were in our new apartment. It was still empty. Airik's apartment was small. We needed to get furniture and other random things. But I loved it. His apartment would never have been ours the way this place was. I appreciated that he had thought of me.

As he walked through the door, I ran and hugged him. When he wasn't home, the days seemed long.

"Hi," he said, smiling and kissing me.

"Hi."

"Did you get the mail? Or maybe there wasn't any?" He pulled off his coat and hung it up. There was one envelope from the mail room - they still used paper for some things here. I hadn't thought to look at it. All my thoughts centered on the assassin. I pulled out the single envelope and read the name on it.

"It's for me?" I frowned.

"Just open it, Quinn."

I tore open the letter and read it. I stared at him.

"What's wrong?" he asked.

"Nothing's wrong. I got in."

"Quinn, that's awesome. Aren't you happy?"

"A little bit." I smiled. "I'm also shocked and scared."

"You're a natural. You're going to do fine."

I certainly hoped so, but I had more important things to think about right now, as my life was in danger. I put the letter down. I had to tell him right away.

"Airik."

He looked up and frowned, sensing something unusual was going on. "What happened?"

"The man from the Sons of the Heavenly Father. He trapped me in the mail room."

"Quinn! I told you not to go out alone." He looked distressed and came to me, looking me over. "Are you all right?"

"I'm all right, Airik. Calm down. He didn't do anything. I chased him away."

"I think you'd better tell me the whole story." He sat down suddenly on the couch.

I explained what had happened before, and how I got so hot I burned my attackers. I told him how I had used the threat to scare away the assassin.

"You turned your thoughts into heat?"

"That's weird, right? Have you heard of anyone being able to do that before?"

"In fairy tales? All the time." Great. Now I was a character from a children's story.

"You say he was afraid?"

"Definitely."

"That's good. It will certainly work in our favor."

When he talked like that, I felt like I wasn't alone.

"I'm going to check with a contact I have with the police and see if they can deport him." He talked for a few minutes with his friend. "They opened an investigation, but there was no real cause for deportation. He's never been charged with a crime."

"Damn," I said. I knew he'd be back, no matter how scared he was.

"He'll be charged with something now."

"What do you mean?" I asked.

"Harassment, Quinn. We have strict laws here. You're not allowed to go around threatening people. We'll be pressing charges immediately. Are you ready to go?"

"I'm ready," I said, a little in awe of my husband. He was someone to fear. It was a dangerous side of him I hadn't seen before.

CHAPTER 9

AIRIK

"Eye luv yoo," I said under my breath in English as I walked down the hall. "How ar yoo too day?"

My digital tutor corrected my pronunciation. I repeated the words, then went on to the next phrase.

"Eye am feen..." The tutor corrected me again. "Eye am fine. Tank yoo."

I sighed. Language study was involved. I tried to commit to memory once again that a 't' and an 'h' together made the sound 'th'.

I wanted to surprise Quinn in a couple of months by being able to speak a little bit of English. It was a slow process. The language was very different from Standard and my mother tongue.

But I would get it. I was determined.

"Eye luv yoo. Fine, tank... thank... yoo."

QUINN

"How did your day go?" Airik asked. I was making dinner when he walked into the kitchen.

I beamed at him.

"It was *amazing*. We worked on opening ourselves to visions, and I had one. Nobody died in it. I still haven't figured out how to separate my personal emotions from the vision."

My instructor's name was Rob. When he wasn't teaching, he led ground teams to rescue potential victims from their future demise. He was teaching my class techniques to protect ourselves from being devastated by our visions. There were ways to put distance between ourselves and what we saw.

"I can help you practice that if you want. I'm the master."

I looked at him and felt hurt creep into my heart. "Yeah, I bet you are."

I looked down at the bread I was piling with meat, vegetables, and cheese.

"What's that supposed to mean?" he said, sounding disgruntled.

I looked up. He had a sour expression on his face. I stayed silent a moment longer but decided to be honest with him. We were supposed to be open with each other, weren't we? Since I had told him about being a psychic, I hadn't kept anything from him.

"I've noticed that you are good at protecting yourself and keeping your distance from people."

He looked mystified.

"You know, not getting close." I turned and stuck a sheet filled with sandwiches into the oven to melt the cheese.

"Not getting close to people in general or not getting close to you?"

"Yes," I said. "You don't let me in. You don't tell me what's wrong when you have a bad day. Remember that Precog you had? The one where you couldn't sleep for a week afterward? You never even told me..."

"That's classified, Quinn. I couldn't discuss it with you."

"You didn't let me finish. What I was going to say was that you never told me how you felt or what you were going through. You pushed me away like I was an annoyance. I thought I was your wife. I'm supposed to help you with your problems."

He stared at me strangely. "I don't need any help."

That was the most hurtful thing he could have said to me. I blinked, trying to breathe through the pain in my chest. He didn't need any help. I knew what he meant. He didn't need me.

"Okay, fine. Duly noted."

I turned away from him and took the sandwiches out of the oven. I slid one onto a plate for him and put the sheet holding the other sandwich back on the stove. As I walked out of the room, Airik turned.

"Aren't you having dinner?"

I stopped and looked back at him, unable to keep the bitterness from my voice.

"I'm not hungry anymore. I have studying to do."

Then I left the room, not able to look at his face for another second, knowing that I was superfluous to him. I was merely an attractive roommate that made it easy to get a fuck when he wanted one. So much for being friends, lovers, and maybe something more. It looked like Airik didn't want anything to do with me.

It hurt more than I had expected.

"Thanks for coming on such short notice, Neesa."

"You made it sound important, so I came right over. I'll do anything for a sister. What do you need?"

I dropped onto the couch and looked up at her. She sat on the opposite arm.

"I want to get Airik's attention."

She let out a big sigh. "He's been pushing you away, hasn't he?"

"He's perfectly polite, Neesa, all the time. I shouldn't complain."

"Do you want polite?"

"No. I want authenticity. The real Airik, not the one he trots out for cocktail parties. I want to know who he is and what concerns him. I want to know what happened that made it hard for him to sleep for a whole week."

Neesa looked at me sympathetically. "I'm sorry, Quinn. He's always been like this. No, I shouldn't say that. He had his heart broken once. After that, all his girlfriends sounded the same. 'He pushes me away.' 'He keeps me at arm's length.' 'He doesn't care about me.' 'He's distant.'"

"Is there a box I can check that says all of the above?" I asked.

She sighed again and sat down beside me. "You poor thing. Airik's a hard nut to crack. I'm sorry."

"It's not your fault, Neesa. I guess he is the way he is. But people change when they desire change. He doesn't want to change right now because everything's great. Why would he want to sabotage the friends with benefits arrangement we have together?"

"Quinn." Neesa put her hand on my shoulder.

"I think I need to shake things up. If this doesn't work and he can't let me in, I'll be taking the divorce option at the end of the year."

Neesa looked shocked. "Did you tell him that?"

"No. I haven't made up my mind yet."

"You sounded pretty sure just now."

"He's making me crazy, and it hurts, Neesa. I want him to see who I am. He doesn't care at all." I stared down at my hands clasped around my knees. "Maybe if he could see me a different way, and through other people's eyes, it would change the way he looks at me. He would know who I am underneath my exterior, and maybe then he would..." I looked down, frowning. "Want me."

Neesa didn't say anything, folding me into a hug. A few tears leaked down my cheeks. I pulled away, standing up.

"I'm not getting upset for no reason. I'm going to do something."

"What's the plan, Quinn? I'm up for it."

I smiled and began to pace as I outlined my idea. "Airik is cut off from his feelings. He's very cerebral. In his head. You know?" Neesa nodded. "I need to get him to feel anything. Once he gets out of his head, maybe he'll start to pay attention to his heart."

"Sounds like a good theory. How are you going to do it?"

"What are some natural feelings to evoke?"

Neesa shrugged.

"Lust, jealousy, anger," I said, counting them off on my fingers.

"That's pretty far from love, Quinn. Don't you want him to love you?"

"I do. But getting him to feel anything will give him access to other, more pleasant feelings, as well."

"You think so?"

"Yep. If not, well, I'll just drive him crazy, which will be a good substitute."

Neesa laughed. "I like the way you think, Quinn. How are you going to elicit those emotions from him?"

"That's not my only goal. It's also about starting to choose my lifestyle instead of being tossed around by current events. I'm going to cut my hair."

"Oh no," she said immediately, a pained look on her face. "Don't cut your beautiful black hair. Please, Quinn. I would kill for hair like that. And besides, women don't wear their hair short on Koccoran."

"That will make me stand out even more. Get used to the idea, Neesa. The hair is going. It's part of my emancipation."

She sighed. "I'll go along with it, but I don't promise to like it."

I smiled. "Okay, then. I want you to help me buy some new clothes that are a little more provocative. I'm going to strut my stuff a bit. I'm sure some alien men exist who will take notice of an off-worlder."

Neesa frowned. "But you won't do anything, right?"

"No!" I said, a little too loudly. Then I lowered my voice. "Of course not. I want Airik. Not any other guy. I would never cheat on him. But he needs to see I am a woman who other men think is sexy. I am a girl who impresses other people. Maybe then he'll be more impressed with me."

"I'm on board so far."

"I think once my training's complete, Rob will offer me a job on his ground team as the on-the-scene Precog. He's been hinting about it. If he does, I'm going to accept."

"You are serious about getting Airik's attention, aren't you?"

"You think he'll be mad?"

"I don't think he will overlook you again."

"What do you want to buy first?" Neesa said, escorting me into one of the empty, airy rooms that filled the shopping mall.

"There's the beach party for Airik's work coming up. I need to get a bathing suit."

She went over to the console and tapped a few times. Immediately ten different kinds of swimsuits appeared in the air before of me. I walked around them, checking them out from all angles. I swiped away all the one-piece swimsuits.

"You're trying to expose as much skin as possible, I see."

"If I'm going to get Airik's attention, I need to be bold, Neesa."

I removed a couple more and tapped in the air on two types I wanted to investigate further. The empty room filled with holograms of the suits. Once I had narrowed it down to a few I wanted to try on, Neesa went to the console. A moment later, the suits came out of the door beside the console. I took them into the changing room at the back and tried them on. The first two didn't work for me. But when I put on the third, I thought it was what I needed.

I walked out of the room and Neesa gasped.

"Do you think it's too much?" I asked.

"Oh, no. That's the one. If it doesn't drive Airik and every man around wild with lust, I don't know what swimsuit will."

"But I don't want to look like a slut."

"You'll see smaller suits than that, trust me. We spend so many months under wraps that once summer comes, people shed their clothes the way a cyx sheds its coat.

The less clothing, the better. Small bathing suits aren't provocative here, not the way they would be on other planets."

"Are you sure?" I repeated, looking at myself in the mirror.

It was an emerald green bikini. There was nothing brash about it, but the triangles that covered my medium-sized round breasts were small. There was a fair amount of my globes left showing which made me uncomfortable, but also made me feel excited and risque. The bottoms were barely there, riding midway between my navel and my sex. In the back, a fair amount of my butt was showing.

It wasn't that it was such a great bathing suit, but more that it looked so good on me. I felt like a sexy woman in it.

"I don't know if I can wear it in public," I said to Neesa.

"That's going to be one of the biggest suits you will see at that party. You're going to knock them dead."

"Okay," I said. "Now how about some sundresses?"

I hadn't expected Airik to dislike my new hairstyle. I liked it. From his grim expression, I knew he didn't feel the same way. I felt as if I had committed a horrendous crime instead of merely hacking off a few lengths of hair.

"It's just a haircut," I said defensively. "I think it looks cute."

"You are the wife of a high-ranking government official on the planet. Women on Koccoran don't wear their hair short."

"You're only worried about your job? Are you kidding me? I got a haircut, Airik. Deal with it."

"Quinn, this isn't just about my job. You don't understand. My career is important to me. I've been working towards this goal for my whole life. I have sacrificed everything to get here. I'm not going to throw it away because you're feeling ignored and throwing a tantrum."

I stared at him. My mouth opened in outrage. I couldn't believe he had the gall to belittle my feelings and pretend my concerns meant nothing.

"Your career means everything? Try talking to your career at the end of the day. I'm sure it will be an excellent listener. Or better yet, try sleeping with your career. Because you're not going to be sleeping with me. You don't care about me, and I don't want to be used for my body. The contract says I don't have to have sex with you unless we both consent. And I don't allow it any more."

"Quinn. You're turning this hair thing into a big fight. What are you upset about?" he said, looking annoyed.

A mirthless laugh escaped me.

"Do you think I'd tell you now?" I said, turning and going into the bedroom. I slammed the door in an attempt to relieve my feelings. It didn't help.

I walked over to the full-length mirror. My hair looked okay, didn't it? I hadn't been sure about cutting it. It used to reach down to my waist, and Airik loved it. By his reaction, he might have loved my hair more than he cared about me. I had worn my hair long all my life. And cutting it had made me more nervous than I had wanted to admit to Neesa.

To be truthful, I had foolishly hoped Airik would think it was beautiful. I turned my head this way and that, looking at myself in the mirror. It looked good. Maybe.

It was a pixie cut. The hairdresser hadn't known what it was. When I showed her a picture, she had said she could do it. She cut both men's and women's hair. At the time, I felt like she had never cut a woman's hair short, but she was willing to make me a pariah if I wanted it. I had felt strong when I was doing it, but now I wasn't sure.

I huffed out my breath and stamped my foot. I had only been married to this guy for a few months. He was already determining my self-esteem and trying to tell me how to wear my hair. I wasn't going to take it.

I gazed into the mirror. My determined blue eyes looked back at me. The pixie cut was combed forward on my head and lay sleek against my skull. A little curl in front of each ear gave me a saucy appearance as if I was really a pixie. I smiled at my reflection.

Coming to this planet was supposed to start a new life for me, but I was wrong. My new hairstyle was a visible symbol of my reinvention, and it was just the beginning. I would show Airik he couldn't ignore me. He couldn't make fun of how I felt.

It didn't matter if I didn't exactly know who I was myself. I was learning as I went along and if he didn't like it, it was too bad for him. I hadn't signed up to be a slave and do whatever he wanted me to. That wasn't in the contract.

I was my own woman.

The next big thing was finishing my training and starting to work with Rob. I could tell that Airik didn't like how well I did in my studies. I thought he would be happy I aced all my classes, but it was making him uncomfortable. Like we were in competition with each other.

I had never wanted to go against him, but if he wanted competition, then he'd get it.

I put on my new bikini with the sundress over it, slapped a floppy sun hat on my head and stalked out of the bedroom.

"Are you ready?" Airik said, stiffly. Apparently we were still fighting. I had no problems with that.

It was time for the staff beach party. He couldn't leave me home by myself. We were going together, even though we weren't getting along.

When we arrived at the beach, we set our things down and laid out towels beside each other. We sat down on them without talking.

"Hi, Quinn!" Rob came running up a big smile on his face. He was in swimming trunks. His chest was broad, and his abs were well-defined. I smiled at him, appreciating the view. He was my teacher and might be my future boss, so I kept my thoughts under control. "Nice hair. Want to come play volleyball?"

I smiled brightly at him. "Sure. It used to be my favorite sport in high school." I turned to Airik, smiling triumphantly. Rob liked my hair. "See you later, honey."

He winced a little at my sarcasm but responded politely. "I'll get you when they're starting the meal."

I nodded, stood up, and pulled off my sundress. I was left standing in my bikini, and both men stared at my body. I kept a smile of satisfaction to myself, but I was pleased with their reaction.

Airik immediately glared at his friend, who grinned at him, then headed over to where they had a beach volleyball net set up. I bounced into the front row, aware of what the motion did to my breasts, and held my hands up ready to set. I glanced over at Airik and saw that he was glowering in my direction.

Good. Let him see what he was missing being such an ass.

I turned to face Rob, who was also in the front row on the other team.

"Ready, Quinn?" he said, a challenge in his voice.

"Let's do it."

CHAPTER 10

QUINN

Today was our three month anniversary. I wondered if Airik even remembered. My attempt to get his attention had ended with us not speaking to each other for a week. That idea wasn't working. I had set aside my troubles with my marriage to concentrate on my training.

I was in a room stuffed with all the other Precog trainees. It was a large space with groups of overstuffed chairs, couches, treadmills, a track for walking that circled the whole room, and a games area.

Everything about the room was designed to help us relax and calm our minds. Visions were difficult to call when your body is tense. Everyone had a different way to decompress. For some people, it was curling up on the couch. For others, it might be going for a walk. Our vision room was identical to the ones trained Precogs used all across Koccoran.

Right now I was practicing recording with the Recorder trainees. Rob gave us a scenario. The Recorders asked us their questions, and we responded as if we were having a vision. The goal was to get us used to the procedure.

Next week, we would be assigned a fully trained Recorder, who would start working with us whenever we had a real vision. As I finished my session with my Recorder, Rob approached us. He leaned over my shoulder and looked at my tablet. I could smell the strong scent of his aftershave.

He smiled at both of us.

"Good work, Quinn. The recording's spot on, too," he told the Recorder. "Quinn, can I have a word with you?"

"Sure," I said, getting up and following him to the track. We began circling the room at a walking pace.

"I wanted to tell you that your training is going very well."

"Thanks," I said reaching up to tuck my hair behind my ear and realizing that there was no hair to tuck any longer. I began to feel nervous. I wasn't sure what he wanted to say to me.

"We've taken into consideration your mature status and your abilities. We've decided to put you on an accelerated program."

I frowned. Mature status? I looked around the room. Everyone else was a teenager or in their early twenties. I knew what he meant, but the way he phrased it made me feel like a grandmother. As for ability, I hadn't noticed that I was any different than the other trainees.

"What do you mean?"

"You're older than these kids. Your skills are already above what any of them will be able to do when they are completely trained. You'll be doing your regular classes but working directly with me as well. We'll be working late every day. The government wants you trained and in the field as soon as possible."

144

"But..."

"Let me put it this way," he said. He stopped and turned to me. "You're the cream of the crop, Quinn. You're at the top of your class. We need your talents out there saving people. This year we had another drop in population. It's important for us to save every person who shouldn't be dying before their time."

"How fast is this going to go? I thought my training would take two years."

"We can do better than that. It's going to be like we're married. Come here at six in the morning. We'll stay until eight at night. We can work on Saturdays. On this schedule, we're hoping to have you working before summer."

"That's only five months away."

"So we better get started now. I want to show you an advanced technique today called memory retrieval."

He headed to one of the glass, sound-proof rooms on the side of a big area used for quiet training sessions. I followed slowly, trying to process what he had said. Was I really so unique I needed a special program? What would Airik think of me spending all this time at school?

We had been growing more and more apart lately. At this point, I didn't care what he thought. I knew right then and there that I wanted this. I wanted to be special. I wanted to be the best Precog I could be. And I wanted to save people.

I was born to do this. If he had a problem with it, he would have to learn how to deal with it.

I got home late that night. The memory retrieval lesson took longer than either of us had expected. It was difficult, but when I finally got the hang of it the feeling had been euphoric.

Now I was exhausted. All I wanted was to go to bed. Airik was working late too. He had messaged me that he would be home in an hour or so and that I shouldn't wait for him. I had a shower and crawled into bed. I didn't even bother to put on pajamas.

I made a fire, and it was scorching in the apartment. I hadn't figured out how to dampen the stove yet. In fact, I didn't put blankets or sheets over my body. I was nearly sweating. The air felt like the heat of summer back home. It comforted me as I fell asleep.

I woke to the feel of a hot, hard body on top of me. A knee spread my legs, and I felt Airik thrust into me. I was wet and aroused, which meant he must have touched me in my sleep before I woke up.

I wanted to be irritated with him. I wanted to sit up and stop him. I said I didn't want to have sex with him anymore, but the feeling of him plunging into me drove every thought except pleasure out of my head. In mere minutes, he had me coming so hard that I cried out. A moment later, he groaned, and I felt his seed filling me.

"Quinn," he said. "I'm sorry you feel like I'm pushing you away. You were right. I'm at keeping my distance." .

He gazed into my eyes, still inside me, his weight pinning me to the bed.

"I don't know what you want this marriage to be, Airik. But if you're going to keep your distance, then we won't know anything about each other. I mean, if that's what you want..."

His eyes looked troubled. "I don't know what I want, Quinn. Even if I want to let you in, I don't know how to change."

The idea popped out of my mouth before I had time to think about it. "We learned something today that helps people with past traumas. It's called memory retrieval. What if I could find the memory that caused you to start pushing people away? You could release it, and you wouldn't do that anymore..."

I trailed off when I saw the outraged expression on his face. He pulled out of me and sat up on the bed, looking down at me like an angry Greek god. He was furious. His chiseled muscles and naked body shook. I had never seen him look angrier before.

"What's wrong?" I asked. I didn't have a clue what I had said that filled him with rage.

"You were learning memory retrieval? Today?"

"Yeah," I said, still confused. "That's why I was late."

147

"Everyone learned it?"

"No. Just me. They're putting me on an accelerated program."

He sat back. "That's interesting."

"Yeah. It was Rob's idea."

"Okay," he said. I knew he still had a problem, but he looked like he wanted to hide his discomfort. "Go to sleep. I'll find out what this is all about in the morning."

"What do you mean? Don't you think I'm good enough to be in an accelerated program? You never even came by to see how I was doing. How would you know my progress?" I said. I hadn't realized it had bothered me until now.

He scowled. "You said you didn't want to ride my coattails. If I showed up there, everyone would know I was your husband and would assume that was the only reason you got in. I was trying to give you space."

"Don't you mean keeping me at arm's length? That's what I'm talking about, Airik. You never asked me if I wanted you to come."

I took a deep breath. All the closeness of the sex had evaporated, leaving us two separate people with a gaping chasm between us.

"I don't know how to be what you want me to be, Quinn," he said.

"That's the problem." I said. "And I also said no sex. Don't do that again."

"Fine. Don't be asleep naked on the bed when I come home anymore."

"Fine," I said.

"I know you enjoyed it, Quinn."

"Yes," I said. "I did. But that's not the point."

"You're right. I'm sorry. It won't happen again unless you ask me."

I knew he meant it. If I wanted him to make love to me again, I was going to have to ask — probably beg. I could deal with that. I didn't plan on doing any begging in the future.

AIRIK

"What are you doing with Quinn's training?" I said, after storming into Rob's office.

He looked up at me calmly. He wasn't upset at all. "She's been placed on an accelerated program."

"Who made this decision?"

"I recommended it, and the head office approved."

"But why?"

"It's not any of your business, Airik, but I'll be straight with you. She's older than the other trainees and far more talented. There's no reason to keep her playing around with them. She could be trained in six months and saving lives in the field."

"Not my business? She's my wife. You know that, Rob. You were at the wedding," I said, glaring at my oldest friend.

"She may be your wife, but she's my student. I make the decisions here. My department isn't yours."

I took a deep breath. I didn't need to piss him off. He would refuse to tell me anything.

"Look. I'm sorry. She's just been driving me crazy lately."

Rob's eyebrows nearly touched his hairline. "A woman has been making you crazy? That's got to be a first," he said, incredulous. "Is this the same guy I went to school with that never got into a fight? Airik the Calm? The one who could never understand what I meant when I told him a girl was making me nuts?"

"You have no idea."

"Oh, I have an idea. You've finally met your match. And you don't know what to do about it, do you?"

He laughed at me. I pressed my lips together and held on to my temper.

"That's what the problem was at the company beach party, wasn't it? You're jealous. "

"I don't know," I said, sighing. "She said she's tired of our friends with benefits arrangement. In fact, she's canceled the benefits part."

Rob's face looked at me with compassion.

"You have no idea of Quinn's capabilities. I don't know what you've been doing during your marriage, but you should pay close attention to her."

"What are you talking about, Rob?"

"She's got a 99.1% accuracy rate already."

I sat down heavily in one of his chairs. "I've been working at this for years, and my accuracy rate is 99.3%. You must have made a mistake."

"I've run the numbers five times, Airik. We based the analysis on over twenty visions. You know that's enough to get a proper baseline."

"How is that possible?"

"I don't know. She's something special."

"She's amazing," I agreed, but my response sounded feeble, even to my ears. Did I know how amazing she was?

"Are we talking about the same woman here, Rob?" I said. "Before she started training, she looked like she was having a seizure when she had a vision. She had no control whatsoever."

"What can I say? I'm an excellent teacher. She certainly doesn't do that anymore. The visions she was having before were child's play. She's a Precog now."

"Already? I can't believe it," I said. "And she's telling me you taught her memory retrieval? That's an advanced technique. She could hurt someone if she does it incorrectly."

"I'm trying to explain it to you, Airik, and you're not getting it. She's a genius. She did two pulls on me, and one on Marla. It only took her fifteen minutes each time."

"Fifteen minutes." I sat back, completely stunned. I was one of the best memory retrievers on the planet. And it took me thirty minutes, sometimes more, to find and retrieve the specific memory I needed.

"You trusted her to pull one of your memories?" I said, not understanding why he would let a rookie do something so dangerous to his mind.

"You are such an idiot, Airik." He shook his head. "I'm your friend. I'm going to tell you something to help you out."

"What?" I said sullenly. I knew I wasn't going to like what came next.

"Quinn is one of the most incredible people I have ever met. She is intelligent, beautiful, intuitive, and frankly the best Precog this training program has ever seen. She's better than me, and she's better than you. She will go on to have an amazing career."

I folded my arms and was silent.

"The question is, are you going to be there with her for it? If she's driving you crazy, if she's trying to get your attention, or if she's upset with you, that means you're not giving her what she needs. In my experience, when women don't get what they need from one man, they go to another and find it."

"Are you saying she would leave me?"

"I'm saying that what a woman needs, a woman needs, no matter their planet of origin. If you don't give it to her, someone else will."

I stood up. "I get it. I appreciate the advice."

"No problem," he said, without a smile.

As I walked out of the building, I knew that Rob had been trying to tell me something. Did he want to take Quinn away from me? He said I needed to take care of her, or else another man would. He was probably right.

What I couldn't figure out was if he wanted to be the other man.

CHAPTER 11

QUINN

I sighed in frustration. The vision was disappearing again as soon I tried to tell my Recorder what I saw. Rob was playing the role of Recorder for me.

"I can't do it," I said, standing up and starting to pace.

"It's fine, Quinn. We've steadily been working for eight hours. It's time for a break."

"No, I want to figure it out. It's one of the most fundamental things I have to learn."

"It's basic, but that doesn't mean it's easy. Imagine rubbing your stomach and patting your head simultaneously. You have to split the activities in your mind and supervise them separately. Once you get it, you'll be able to do it forever. You just have to figure it out first. Can you tap your head and pat your stomach?" he said, demonstrating.

I blinked, looking at him like he was crazy. "I don't know."

"Did you ever play a musical instrument?" he asked, not phased by my facial expression at all. "It's the same thing, being able to read and play at once."

"No, I didn't." I put one hand on my stomach and one on my head. I started patting my head, but as soon as I tried to rub my belly, my hands got confused.

"This is stupid," I said. I scowled at Rob. "You make it look easy."

"It will be easy when you get it. All you need is practice. Once you understand, it will become second nature for you. Until then, it's hard."

"Hard? It feels impossible, Rob."

"Calm down. You've been working long hours for the past few months."

"Right. I've put in the hours, but I still can't do a basic thing. I need to be able to do this if I'm going to work for the Precog Division, Rob. It's important to me."

"Quinn, you're not going to learn anything if your brain is starved and exhausted. Let's grab something to eat and I'll take you home."

I stared at him, feeling defeated. I wanted to practice more, but I knew lesson time was over. "Okay."

Dressing for the cold was second nature by now. I pulled on my mitts and adjusted my scarf as Rob and I walked out into the darkening afternoon. The snow was falling. A strong wind blew into our faces. I winced. It was only the beginning of my second winter.

We headed down the street. Rob waited outside while I ducked into the restaurant. I wanted to grab something for dinner. When I came back out, Rob turned and headed for my apartment.

"When this training session is over, I'll be returning to the field."

"That will be more interesting for you, right?"

"No, I like working with trainees. Field work is sometimes annoying and challenging. It's even lonely, if you can imagine it."

He stared at me, looking deeply into my eyes. I was surprised. Was Rob interested in me as more than his student? The idea bothered me and made me feel guilty even though I hadn't done anything wrong.

"Why do you do it then?" I asked, trying to break the tension.

"I like variety in my life. This way I get to save people instead of just talking about it."

"Right." I nodded. Where was this conversation going?

"The reason I'm telling you is because when I go back out, I want you on my team."

"As part of your group?" I said, flabbergasted. I thought he might try to recruit me, but I hadn't expected an offer as soon as today. I had thought he might ask me. But I hadn't expected him to ask me so soon.

"Nothing's definite yet. I just wanted to let you know what I was thinking. If everything goes to plan, I can make you an official offer as soon as you get your certification. I'm putting my team together now."

"Thanks, Rob. I feel honored. But why would you want a newbie on your team?"

"I realize everything is new to you, but you have the potential to be one of the most powerful Precogs I've ever known. I only want to work with the best."

"Rob, I can't even report and keep my vision running at the same time," I said, feeling myself turn red under my scarf.

He stopped and turned my body to face him. "You'll get it. Don't worry, Quinn. I'm not lying about you being one of the best."

I rolled my eyes. "Better than you? Better than Airik?"

"I have never seen anyone learn as quickly as you do. You are intuitive and connected. You're unbelievable, Quinn, and don't let anyone tell you differently."

I had the sense that when he said anyone, he meant Airik. Not that Airik ever directly put me down, but he made me feel small when it came to anything about mental abilities. I suppose he thought he was better due to his training. Rob was making me feel special.

I could see on Rob's face that he was struggling with something. He took me by surprise when he kissed me on my face, where my third eye was. A vision flashed through my head, and I slowed the pictures down. I was able to follow my lessons!

Rob and I training more. Me getting the ability to report and have a vision at the same time. Rob hugging me. Rob and I in the field and him making advances. Me resisting over and over. And then one night...not resisting. Rob and I finally making love.

I pulled away and stepped back, feeling upset.

"I'm sorry. I shouldn't have done that," he said. "You're Airik's wife. I don't know what I was thinking."

"No, no. It's fine. It was platonic, right?" I said, unsure if that was true or not. I glanced up at our window and wondered if Airik had seen us together. I hoped he wasn't home yet.

"I don't know what that means. You were upset. I was trying to comfort you." It sounded as if he were attempting to convince himself as much as me.

"It shouldn't happen again, Rob," I said.

"No, it won't. It was unprofessional of me, Quinn. I won't let it happen again. I swear."

"Long life, Rob," I said and gave him a wave as I turned and went into our apartment building. I had a flash of how it felt when he made love to me, and I wondered what the vision meant.

LISA LACE

Later that night, I was sitting on the couch and studying when Airik came in. "Hello," I said, not looking up at him.

"Hey," he said, his voice sounding exhausted.

I glanced up when I heard his voice. His eyes looked as though he hadn't slept well for some time. I felt badly for us, but he was the one who had pushed us apart. We barely spoke to each other now. We hadn't made love in ages. I was longing for him, but I wouldn't give in. If we could only make this work on a physical level, the sex had to come to a stop, too. I needed more than just good sex and a friendly roommate. Not that we were particularly friendly these days, either.

I sighed and went back to my studying. I expected him to go to the kitchen or the bedroom. Instead, he came and sat down beside me.

"What are you studying?" he said. His leg was so close to mine that our knees touched. I positioned myself so we weren't adjacent anymore. I didn't need to get distracted.

"History of the first Precogs. How the cold and their diet of fatty meat helped create the parts of the brain to develop these mental abilities."

"Ah." He nodded.

Unbidden, I remembered the vision of Rob and me making love. A shot of guilt went through me. He frowned immediately.

"What's wrong?"

"What do you mean?" I said, looking away.

"You're feeling guilty."

I had forgotten he was an empath. I made it my next order of business to get better at shielding and learn how to keep my thoughts and feelings from Airik. The thought that I wanted to protect myself from him made me sad. But he had put us here. Not me.

"Why are you feeling guilty, Quinn? What have you done? Is it with Rob? Did you cheat on me?" His face turned red, and he looked angry. I thought I was going to cry. How had we ended up here? When we had got married, we both had high hopes for the future.

"I can't believe you would accuse me of something like that. I didn't do anything," I said, but the vision of Rob and me popped into my head again. I felt the guilt rising inside me, and I knew he did as well.

"When you say that, I feel your guilt increasing, but you're not lying."

"Rob kissed me today." Airik cursed under his breath. "On the forehead, Airik. It was entirely platonic. I was upset because I was having problems with the training."

"So he kissed you on the forehead? Seems like an unusual teaching approach."

"He was comforting me. I didn't ask him to. I'm not interested in Rob." But I might be sometime in the future, I thought to myself.

"There's the guilt again."

"When he kissed my third eye, I had a vision."

"What did you see?" He looked troubled.

"I saw Rob and I having sex," I blurted out, not meeting his eyes.

"When?" Airik ground out.

"Just a moment," I said, accessing the memory of the vision, dropping into it and looking for time markers. I popped out of my mind again with the information.

"What did you just do?" he said with a frown.

"I didn't get a timeframe on the vision, so I went back and found out when it was going to happen."

"You didn't get the timeframe when the vision was happening?"

"No, I was upset. I wasn't paying attention to everything. I'm still in training!" I said, feeling defensive.

"How did you get the timeframe now?"

"It's a different procedure I figured out, but it's pretty accurate. I remember the vision and drop into it."

"You drop into it? What does that even mean?"

"I play again as if it's happening for the first time."

He looked at me, utterly bewildered. "You can do that?"

"Can't everybody?"

He shook his head.

"It works for me. When it's playing again, I look for the time markers like they taught me at school."

He stared at me, arms crossed as if he couldn't figure me out.

"Is that wrong or something?" I said, unsure what he was upset about this time.

"It's not wrong, exactly. But I'm not the only one who can't replay their visions. I've never heard of anybody being able to do that. Why do you think we have Recorders?"

"Well, um, I don't know what that means," I said, changing the subject back to Rob. "But I have the timeframe, and it's about a month and a half from now." A couple weeks after our possible divorce date, which was looking more and more likely considering the way our relationship was going.

"You're going to sleep with him."

I frowned. "No. I have no desire to have sex with Rob."

"Not now," he said, accusing.

"Not ever. I don't care about Rob."

"That's not how it looks. You had a vision, Quinn," he said, standing up and glaring at me.

I felt frustrated and angry. I took a moment to gather my thoughts, and then I stood up and raised my voice.

"You told me that visions can be changed," I said, stepping closer to him. "If the vision comes to pass, Airik, why do you think that would happen?" I felt tears rush to my eyes as I struggled to control my emotions.

He gave me a piercing look. I saw hurt, anger, and jealousy in his eyes.

"I'll give you a hint," I said. "If it ever happened, it would be because I was so unhappy with you that I had no other choice to get my needs met."

All the color drained out of his face. He sat down quickly as if his legs wouldn't hold him.

"I don't want it to be like this between us," I said. I sat down beside him, my voice sounding anguished to my ears. "But you're pushing me away. I can't fix it. Only you can."

He scrubbed a hand across his face.

"But how?" he said, his voice sounding as desperate as I felt. "How can I fix it, Quinn? I want to."

I thought for a moment. "What happened to you in high school when your heart got broken, Airik? We have to find the memory so that you can face it and release it. Maybe you will be free from your trauma then."

"It wasn't a trauma," Airik whispered.

"Anything that hurts you enough to scar your psyche and prevent you from being happy is traumatic. I'd say this qualifies."

I studied him. "You'd have to let me do a memory pull on you. Honestly, I don't think you trust me enough to do that, Airik." He looked at me but didn't deny what I'd just said. "If you let me do that, it would show me that you cared about us and about fixing what's wrong between us."

"I can't imagine letting you do a memory pull on me," he said. He looked like I had suggested he get a frontal lobotomy.

"I've done over ten already," I said.

"Ten? At school? Why would Rob have you do memory pulls already?"

"It wasn't at school," I said. "Not officially. Word got around that I'm kind of good at them. People started asking me for help."

"Are you serious?"

"Airik, I know you're my husband. You care about me in your own way. I'm sorry, but you have no idea what's going on with me. You don't know how I'm doing in school because you never ask me. You don't know what troubles or worries me. I assume you don't care, or you're busy with your own work. You don't even know little things, like I fell on the ice today and hit my head. You're not interested in my life."

"You fell on the ice? Did you have it checked?"

I laughed.

"You're missing the point. You would never have known if I hadn't deliberately mentioned it. You don't ask me about myself. You want to have sex with me, and you say you want to get past this problem in our relationship, but I have to ask you a simple question. Why?"

He stared at me helplessly.

"If you don't think I'm an interesting person, what's the point? You can get sex from any woman. You're a celebrity on this planet and incredibly good-looking. You don't need me, Airik. We can finish out our time and get divorced."

"Quinn…"

"Airik," I gazed at him sadly. "I think we both hoped this might turn into something more, but it's not working out. I think we should let it go."

"Quinn, please."

I shook my head. I had nothing more to say.

When Airik and I were shopping for groceries in silence the next day, I got a bad feeling. There was a dull sense of dread in the pit of my stomach, and I looked around, wondering what the threat was. Airik glanced at me. I knew he had picked up on my emotions. He looked alert and was searching for the danger as well.

But nothing happened.

We finished getting the groceries, paid and took the food out of the store to a car waiting for us outside. Everything felt peaceful until, without warning, a man ran up to us and grabbed me. He threw me into a different vehicle and jumped in after me.

Airik had been on the other side of our car, loading it with groceries. We were gone before he could get around to the sidewalk.

In our car, my abductor moved as far away from me as he could get, all the way to the other side. He was scared of me.

"Do you think you're going to get away with this?" I said. "My husband's coming after us right now."

I hoped he was.

"It will only be a few minutes. We'll near a place I can burn you safely," he said, and I stared at him. How did a person get so fucked up?

"Why don't you shoot me instead?" I said. In retrospect, this wasn't the most profound question I could have asked at the time, but I had wondered about the tactics of Sons of the Heavenly Father.

"Witches must be burned. Our scriptures say so. Killing you is my first assignment. To go back to Earth, I must have proof of your death. Without proof, my life will be forfeit."

I wasn't genuinely frightened until he spoke. I started to get scared then because the man seemed completely unhinged. I was alone in a car with a maniac, and I didn't know where I was going.

Before I knew it, the car stopped, and we were getting out in a field near an abandoned building. Whoever this person was, he came prepared. There was a platform set up with wood around the bottom, all ready for me. The only thing missing was an audience of people screaming "BURN HER!" I started to shake then. Terror gripped my soul.

He was going to kill me. Not with a little bullet to the head, either. He was going to burn me alive. He yanked me out of the car and over to his construction, tying me securely despite my struggles. I tried to summon my internal fire. I didn't know how it happened before, and I couldn't do it now.

I twisted and pulled at the ropes holding me to the stake, but my captor was good with knots. I tried to breathe slowly. I felt myself hyperventilating. Soon I saw spots in front of my eyes. I felt myself going unconscious.

I was glad there wasn't a crowd of people to see me. This wasn't what a strong woman in charge of her destiny would do at all — faint.

But at least I would be unconscious when I burned to death. That was good, wasn't it? I didn't think that I would get to find out. Before I could wake up, I would be dead.

AIRIK

When I saw the car speeding away with Quinn in it, my reaction wasn't to race after her. I sat down in the car and calmed my fear and anger. My emotions wouldn't save Quinn. I had to rescue her, no matter how angry she was with me. It was my job to keep her safe.

I closed my eyes and did exercises that took me into a deeper state of consciousness until I felt completely relaxed. Then I called a vision. I focused on Quinn and opened myself.

There.

She was tied to a stake as flames licked at her legs. I fought against the panic that lurked on the edges of my mind. My years of training was the only thing preventing me from losing control. Carefully, I committed the place and time of the vision to memory. Then I let it go and came back to reality.

It only took me a moment to find the coordinates of the empty factory I had seen in the Precog. I programmed them into the car, and it took off at the highest possible speed.

I was acting recklessly. Being careful and cautious was my usual style. But I didn't have much time. The faster I got to Quinn, the sooner I could intervene on her behalf. She would die in less than twenty minutes. I had no time to waste.

When I got to her, the assassin was kneeling beside Quinn. He was preparing to light a fire around her. I wondered why he didn't use a more efficient method of dispatching people, but I was thankful for it now because it meant I still had time to save her.

I ran up to her captor. He was so intent on what he was doing that he didn't hear me or look up. I kicked him in the stomach and grabbed his head, slamming it hard into my knee. He groaned. I pushed him aside, pulling out a knife and cutting the ropes that tied Quinn to the stake. She moved away from the fire that had started to burn her pants. I took her hand.

"No!" The sound of the man's howl made us both look at him. He had recovered quickly and was running at us with a knife in one hand and a gun in the other. I felt Quinn tense up beside me. I wanted to run, but she stood firm and lifted her hand.

He screeched to a halt so comically that I would have laughed if the situation hadn't been dangerous. I looked over at her and watched as heat waves moved through the air from her hand towards the man, melting both the gun and the knife.

I couldn't believe it. I had never seen a Precog do that before. But already I was beginning to suspect that Quinn was something more than an ordinary Precog.

"No, please don't," he said, turning and running towards a pile of trash. Quinn followed him, wielding her hot hand. The next thing I saw in my mind was a vision of an explosion.

"Quinn, stop!" I shouted. As I said the words, I knew I was too late.

The man ran and hid behind the rubbish. Quinn's fist followed him and hit a barrel full of gas fumes. She heated them up and created an explosion, releasing all the energy from the barrel. Her hand was hot enough to ignite something. We were blown back from the shock wave. Quinn was unharmed, of course, but my head was bleeding.

It took us a minute for us to recover. When we did, Quinn looked at me — aghast. "What have I done?" she said.

"You didn't do anything. It was an accident," I said. I went to investigate the body, but there was almost nothing left. I came back to her and pulled her away to the car.

"It's over, Quinn," I said. "He's gone. No one is looking for you anymore. You can relax."

She nodded at me, still in shock. "Yes, he's certainly gone."

Both of us wondered how Quinn had changed her future.

CHAPTER 12

QUINN

The first day of my new Precog job was long and tiring. I crawled into bed as quietly as I could to let Airik sleep. I pulled the covers around me and curled up into a ball. I smiled to myself, thinking back over the events that led me here.

It was the first time I felt happy since the day of my kidnapping. The same day, I had inadvertently killed my would-be assassin. The questioning from police and paperwork had been horrible. Thank goodness it was all over now. I was not going to let his memory ruin my first pleasant day at work.

The first time I was able to report and not lose track of the vision was a long time ago. Rob ran out of the room, and my class had cheered. We always applauded when people first communicated successfully with their Recorder because it was arduous. At the time, it was the best moment of my life. Everyone smiled at me or clapped. A few had yelled my name. For the first time, I felt like I belonged somewhere.

I wriggled around, feeling like I was going to burst with happiness. I thought back to when I had received my certification. All my hard work and practice had paid off. I was an official Precog, and I would soon be working with the best of the best. I couldn't wait. I was ready to go out and save people.

When I received my certificate, I had a vision of my future. There was a much older version of me, giving a retirement speech after a long and successful career with the Precog Division. That's when I knew I was where I was supposed to be.

Airik had welcomed me to the Division, along with other new hires. He hadn't treated me any differently from anyone else. I knew now that the divorce was going to go through. Our marriage wasn't going anywhere. He had never asked me to do the memory pull, which meant he didn't trust me to do it. He didn't care enough to try and save our relationship.

The thought made me sad, but I had accepted the idea of life without him. He already was only with me physically, not with his mind.

"What are you squirming around for?" Airik's voice came from the other side of the bed. I froze.

"I'm sorry. I didn't mean to wake you," I said. Maybe we should have separate beds. It would make more sense. But I hadn't been able to give up the notion of sex just yet. It was the only thing that had ever really worked with us. We hadn't slept together for quite a while, but moving into another room had seemed so final that I hadn't been able to make myself do it.

"It's okay. Are you having problems sleeping?"

"I was thinking about today," I said. I was also surprised we were having a conversation.

"How was it?"

"It was fantastic," I smiled to myself in the darkness. "Overwhelming and challenging. But overall, it was good. Splendid."

He chuckled. "That sounds like my first day with the Division, too. I haven't always been this confident, Quinn."

"That's hard to believe," I said.

I felt him turn onto his side. "Give me your hand, Quinn."

I reached out in the darkness, and he clasped hands with me. I gasped as his first day played through my mind.

Airik's fear, worry, and nerves. His joy at finally achieving his dream. Airik's attraction for a woman working in his unit. Airik celebrating with his friends — Rob among them — after the momentous day was over.

He had sent me his memories. It was a complicated technique that people typically learned on the job, but I had already mastered it during my training. Airik didn't let go after the thought push was over. I didn't pull my hand away. I enjoyed the comfort of his touch. We had been apart for a long time.

"I've missed you," he whispered, pulling my hand to his lips and kissing the back of it. I felt a sizzle of desire go through me.

I didn't answer him. Of course, I wanted to sleep with him as much as he wanted to have sex with me. But was it right? Then the realization dawned on me that it didn't matter. We wouldn't be staying married after our divorce, so what happened now made no difference at all. If we were trying to fix things, I would want to hold out until he gave me his heart before I resumed our physical relationship.

But now? Now it didn't matter. I had no hope of him ever letting me in, so I was free to fuck him as much as I wanted. In a short time, we would be miles apart. I would never see him again. I felt like crying at the thought, but that was how it had to be. The fact that it meant I could have sex with Airik again lessened the pain.

He sighed and pulled his hand from mine. I felt him roll away, turning his back to me. Then I realized that I had never answered his comment. Shit. He thought I was still mad. He thought I was rejecting him.

I didn't need to let him think those thoughts any longer. I drew in a deep breath and got out of bed.

"Quinn?" I heard his sad voice. "Please don't go."

"I'm not going anywhere," I said, pulling my nightgown over my head and dropping it on the floor. I shimmied out of my panties and crawled back into bed.

"Oh," he said, sounding confused. "Sleep well then."

I swallowed and gathered my courage, hoping he wouldn't push me away. "Sleeping wasn't what I had in mind," I said, pressing my naked body up against his. He was only wearing boxers, as usual. His hard chest heaved under my hands as he realized that I was willing again.

"Quinn? Are you sure?"

I slid my hand down into his underwear and grasped him, smiling when I heard his gasp of surprise.

"Yes, Airik. I'm sure."

"Then say it."

"Say what?"

He didn't answer me. He just waited. I huffed out my breath. He had said that he wouldn't make love to me again unless I asked him.

"Will you make love to me, Airik?"

"I thought you'd never ask." He leaned towards me, whispering in my ear and making me shiver.

I pulled my hand away, and he rolled over, pinning me underneath him. I was having trouble breathing, but I loved the feeling of him being in control. I was tired of being the one making all the decisions. I wanted to let him be in charge.

He bent down and claimed my lips, and I opened to him immediately, finding his tongue and twining mine with his. He rolled us both to the side so he could keep kissing me while fondling my breasts. My nipples were sensitive after such a long stretch with no stimulation. I moaned into his mouth. I felt him push his hips towards me, his hardness pressing into my thigh.

He played with them for a long time until I needed more. I broke the kiss, sucking in air, and begged him. "Airik, please."

Airik bent his head and took one of the tight buds into his hot mouth. I drew in a deep breath, feeling my hips buck. I loved this. He was good at making love to me. At least, that was one thing we had right between us.

I felt the urge to touch him for a change. I pushed him, rolling him onto his back again.

"Quinn?" he asked, but I was already on top of him, kissing and licking my way down his body. His breath came in short gasps. I brushed his cock as I moved down. I kissed his belly and cupped his balls, loving the feel of them in my hand.

I dropped my head and took him in my mouth. He groaned. I had never done that to him before. I had never done it to any man. But I wanted him to experience pleasure with me. I wanted to make him happy, even if he didn't love me. I moved up and down on him until he finally pushed me away.

"Did I do it wrong?" I said, a little mortified. Maybe I should have asked how to do it properly.

"If you keep that up, I'm going to come."

"Oh," I said in a small voice, smiling to myself.

"Come here," he said, and I crawled back up. He maneuvered me until I straddled him, and then he lifted me up and over him. I spread wide and lined him up with my sex. I eased myself slowly down onto him until our hips were flush. It took a while because I needed to stop and breathe and let my body adjust to him.

"Airik," I said, lifting myself and dropping back down again. He breathed out heavily. I rode him hard until I couldn't stand it anymore. I arched my back as the orgasm rocked me. I jerked violently, my body wracked with bliss. And through the haze of ecstasy, I felt him stiffen and fill me. For a moment, I wished I would get pregnant and take something of him with me when I left the planet. The thought was crazy. I needed to be careful what I wished for.

Finally, I lay still with my head on his chest. He was still deep inside me. I didn't want him to pull out. I knew then that I loved Airik. More than life, more than anything.

"I love you," I whispered in English.

"Lights," he murmured. Indirect lights sprang to life, making us visible to each other.

"What are you saying, Quinn?" he said, in Standard, kissing my sweaty cheek as I lifted my head. I looked at him and smiled, unable to keep the love from my gaze.

"Nothing important. It's a common expression from back home."

"What was it again?"

I hesitated for a moment. But what could it hurt to tell him? He would never know what it meant. "I love you," I said again.

He studied me with an odd look on his face. "Just an expression?" he said.

"Pretty much."

He kissed me again. We lay twined up together, kissing. I didn't want the feeling of closeness to end.

"Why did you do this, Quinn?" he whispered.

I frowned. "I wanted to. Didn't you?"

"Of course. But you said something different before."

"Oh. That's right." I looked away from him and felt the distance come between us again.

"Did something change?"

I pulled myself away from him. The cold air hit my sweaty, naked body and chilled me.

"I thought that since we'll be getting divorced in a couple of weeks, it didn't matter what we did or didn't do."

His face fell, and my heart cracked. "You want to get a divorce?"

"Don't you?" I said, my voice full of pain. "I'm nobody. You don't know which planet I'm from because you never asked. I'm bothering you, cutting my hair, and

180

making you jealous. I'm a big pain in your ass, Airik. Don't pretend I'm not. I'm sure you are counting the days until we can get divorced."

He looked at me, still shocked. "I hadn't considered it a possibility."

"Because things were going so well between us? I can't do this anymore. You've kept me at arm's length since the beginning. You don't trust me. You don't want me, except for sex."

"Quinn."

I went on as if he hadn't spoken. "You don't love me, Airik. I thought I could live in a marriage without love, but it's harder than I imagined. I'm sorry, but I don't see what else there is for us to do."

I started to get out of bed. He put his hand on my arm to stop me.

"Wait, Quinn. There's something I need to tell you. It's part of the reason I push you away."

I turned around and met his gaze, which was honest and bare. I felt like he was showing himself to me for the first time.

"I had a vision of the woman that I would fall in love with."

"You knew who your true love was, but you still married me?"

"I saw her death, Quinn." He swallowed hard and looked so pained it hurt my heart. "I couldn't tell the particular time, but she might be dead already."

"She isn't me," I said. "Now your behavior makes more sense."

"I don't know if she isn't you because I don't know who she is. I didn't see her face. My vision was interrupted. I'm fairly confident she can't be you."

"Why not?"

"Because the woman wasn't Koccoran. She was from…" he hesitated, not wanting to tell me. "She was from Earth. She was a human."

He looked ashamed of the fact that his true love was supposed to be a human. I rolled my eyes. Were we insignificant to these stuck-up Koccorans?

"She was human. Like me." I said. I got out of bed and grabbed my clothes, putting them on with jerky movements. "Didn't Kartar tell you anything about me? I guess this cements our divorce now. You couldn't possibly stay married to a human."

I looked up from putting on my socks when I became aware of his silence. Airik stared at me.

"You're human?"

"Airik, the company is called *TerraMates*. Where do you think they get all the women? For someone who thinks he's so smart, you can be pretty dumb sometimes. Do you want a divorce right now?"

He got up and pulled me back to the bed.

"You're not what I expected a human to be. In fact, I thought you were Susohnnan."

"If you meant to compliment me, you just failed."

"It doesn't matter that you're human, Quinn. I care about you. I don't want to divorce you."

"But what about your true love? It looks like you married a human, but not the right one."

He looked tormented.

"Have you told anyone about your vision?" I said, feeling compassion rising in me despite myself.

"Not really."

"You know how that bothers you," I said, chiding him.

He looked surprised.

"Come on. Every time you have a big vision, you can't sleep for days. Just like me. But to see your true love die..." I stopped the train of thought before I told him that I had a similar vision. "It must be horrible."

"It was." He stared down at his strong hands, clenching them into fists.

183

"Do you want to tell me about it?" I asked. I held my breath and wondered what he would do. Would he make light of everything and push me away again? Or would he confide in me?

"No." My heart dropped into my shoes. I got up to finish getting dressed, but he grabbed my arm again to stop me.

"Airik," I barked. He still wasn't going to let me in.

"I don't want to, but I think I should."

He looked up at me. It felt like he was showing me his real self for the first time. Tears started to fill my eyes.

"She was driving at night. With an older man. It was her father, I think. She was scared. Someone was following them. People wanted to hurt her."

I frowned.

"They decided to go to a police station. The police stations on Earth are different than ours. They let some bad things happen, and they only came out when it was too late to protect her."

"What things?" I said, feeling lightheaded. This story seemed familiar.

"Her father said she should make a run for it. She ran right to the door. She almost got in, but someone..." He was getting choked up. "Someone shot her," he managed to get out.

I put my hand up to the scar. "Was it in the neck, right here?"

"How do you know that?" He couldn't take his eyes off my neck as I rubbed at the scar.

"The woman was me."

CHAPTER 13

AIRIK

My legs were heavy, and I couldn't move. I was stunned. How could Quinn be the woman from my vision? I thought I was shocked when she told me she was human. But she was still speaking. Her face was filled with emotion. I tried to pay attention to her.

"I was conscious, but my body wouldn't respond. Some men picked me up and carried me down the street. My father wanted to get help, but someone held a gun to his head, so he wasn't able to do anything."

She gazed off into space as she saw everything in her mind's eye again.

"I was angry and frustrated. I had been bothered my whole life for being myself. People had hurt me and said cruel things to me before. These guys were in a different league altogether. They thought I was a witch. They were going to burn me."

Though I already knew bits and pieces of this story, I was filled with horror at the thought of what happened to Quinn. I hadn't been entirely wrong about humans.

"My skin started burning up. My body was so hot that I started to hurt him."

"You mentioned that before. Somehow you turned your emotions into heat?"

"Something like that. They dropped me. That's where my father and the police found me. After that, Dad convinced me to use TerraMates to get off Earth. They wouldn't have stopped until I was dead. They didn't stop. But we stopped them, I guess." I pulled her into my arms as she shook, remembering terrible things.

"My vision was interrupted," I murmured. "That's why I thought she...you...had died."

"But Airik," she said, sitting back and looking up at me. I could tell she didn't want to hope for our future. "What does it mean if I'm the woman from your vision?"

I rubbed my hands over my face, trying to come to terms with everything I had just learned.

"I don't know, Quinn."

She nodded. The light in her eyes flickered out. I knew I had given the wrong answer.

"I know what it means," she said, looking devastated. "It means that even though I'm supposed to be the one for you..."

Her eyes were filled with tears again, and one rolled down her cheek.

"You still don't love me," she said, getting up and running to the bathroom.

I didn't stop her because it was true.

QUINN

I knocked on Neesa's apartment door and waited.

"Quinn?" She took one look at my tear-stained face and pulled me inside. "What's wrong?"

"Just about everything," I said, my voice breaking.

"Wash your face. I'll make us a cup of tea, and you can tell me the whole story," she said, heading to the kitchen.

I went into her bathroom and splashed cold water on my face. When I went back out, I huddled up in a corner of the couch. I took off my shoes and pulled my knees up to my chest, feeling minuscule.

Neesa came back and handed me a delicate china teacup with a beautiful blue rose on it. "Now, what's going on?" she asked, sitting down in a chair across from me.

"Airik." I stopped, feeling tears coming again. I took a trembling breath and tried to calm myself.

"I should have known it would be him. What has the big oaf done now? You know I love him, Quinn. But he's not the best at relationships. Tell me what he did and I'll kick his ass."

That got a tiny smile out of me, but it disappeared immediately.

"It's not just him, Neesa. We're not working. Do you remember how I tried to get his attention? That just made him upset. He hasn't let me in until today. He told me about a woman he's supposed to fall in love with."

"Yes, I've heard about that too. The human."

"As it turns out, I'm the woman." I watched her, wondering if there would be an adverse reaction.

She frowned. "You can't be. I always thought you were Susohnnan."

I laughed. "That's what Airik said. Doesn't anyone on this planet know the origin of the word Terra in TerraMates?"

"But you're sophisticated. How can you be human?"

"Maybe humans aren't what you thought they were."

"I'm not prejudiced," she said, holding up her hands. "But that means that you're his true love. Isn't this good news? It's what you wanted, isn't it?"

"But Neesa," I said, feeling my tears spilling out again. "He doesn't love me. I can see it in his eyes. When the year is up, I'm filing for divorce."

"Divorce." She stared at me. All traces of amusement vanished from her face. "Why would you want to do that?"

"He doesn't love me, and I know now he never will," I said, crying in earnest now. "It's stupid to keep trying when it's not going to work."

"I agree that it doesn't make sense to keep pushing something that isn't going to happen. But Quinn, you can't give up. He had a vision he would love you." She took my hand and put her other hand on top. "Airik's visions are incredibly accurate."

"Not this time, Neesa. I'm one of the mistakes."

She looked at me with an eyebrow raised.

I smiled. "You're right. It wasn't a mistake. In many ways, this has been the best year of my life. Now that I have Koccoran citizenship, I'm staying. This is the only place I've ever fit in. And having you for a sister, well..." I started crying again.

"That's right," she said. Her eyes were tear-filled as well. "Even if you divorce my idiot brother, we're still going to be sisters. I'm not giving you up."

"You already have a lot of sisters, Neesa," I said.

"None of them are pale little human Precogs that have blown up Precog testing machines."

I shook my head. "I didn't destroy that machine. It was going to break eventually. It needed maintenance."

"Whatever you say. The way I hear it, you're one of the most powerful Precogs the Division's ever seen."

"I'm going to focus on my career. That will have to make me happy."

"You're going to knock them dead at the Division," she said, putting her arm around my shoulder. "Are you crashing here tonight or are you going home?"

"I guess I'll go back. Airik might be worried. I didn't tell him where I was going."

"He'll be freaking out." she said, frowning at me. "I'm contacting him right now to tell him you're here and okay, but I'm also saying you are leaving to go home now. He may not love you, but he cares about you, Quinn. Don't worry him for no reason."

"I'm sorry," I said, feeling contrite. I grabbed my cold-weather clothes and got dressed. When I returned home, Airik was at the door the moment I walked through the threshold.

"Quinn, please don't worry me like that again. I didn't know where you'd gone or if something had happened to you." His eyes were troubled. "You were so upset when you left."

I stared at him and knew that his heart was hurting nearly as much as mine was. He swept me up into his arms and kissed me until I felt like I was going to melt into a puddle on the floor.

"Please, Quinn. Let me show you how I feel," he said, his eyes begging for forgiveness.

I didn't say anything, but I nodded my head. Sex was the only way we could get close to each other. I wouldn't fight it again. I loved him. I wanted him to make love to me and help me forget all the pain I felt.

It was slow, passionate, and exquisitely pleasurable. I thought I would explode before he would let me come. When my orgasm finally hit me, the mind-numbing sensation seemed like it would never end. Finally, we both lay still, our bodies twisted up together.

"Have you ever had an orgasm like that before, Quinn?" he whispered.

"Never," I said, almost unable to form words.

"Me neither," he said.

Then I saw a change come over his face.

"What is it?" I said.

"A vision's coming." He started to untangle himself, but it was too late. His eyes were looking right at me, but he didn't see me. In a different voice, he activated his computer to call his Recorder.

"Precog," he said.

I lay still. I couldn't move now, or I might break his vision. At that moment, I felt a vision coming to me. "Precog." I activated my computer and called my Recorder. After that, I was lost in the Precog.

I was walking by myself in a snowy forest that seemed vaguely familiar. I came to a log cabin. I had been sent to help a woman who was sick. I was a nurse. Her daughter had just died. The woman was hysterical and running a fever. She hadn't been able to give any details because she was too distraught. We had barely been able to get her coordinates before we lost contact.

The silence in the cabin was stifling. The girl and her mother were already dead. I walked over to the bedroom and saw the two lying side by side. My stomach heaved. I got to work, preparing to bring them back on the stretcher I pulled behind me. The cabin was deep in the northern mountains, far from any towns. I packed up the bodies and headed back to civilization.

The vision jumped ahead. I was dying in the hospital where I worked. My supervisor was asking me to tell her everyone I had contacted.

"Keela, we need to quarantine them. It's important."

My supervisor looked frantic, but I felt as hot as a volcano. Whatever she needed to know didn't matter.

"Please try and remember," she said, but my eyes closed.

I knew she was dead then, but the Precog went on. Millions of people would die of the same disease the nurse contracted. The planet-wide catastrophe could end the whole Koccoran race.

Suddenly I was back in my body. My Recorder's voice kept asking me questions, drawing more and more details out of me until I couldn't answer anymore.

"That's great, Quinn," she said. "Would you mind coming into Headquarters as soon as you have dressed?"

"Right now?"

"Yes. We need to speak with you and Airik."

"Okay," I said, feeling curious.

I opened my eyes and looked into Airik's. We were still intimately wrapped around each other. The feeling of him inside me made my hips buck.

"If you do that again, Quinn, we're not going to make it to Headquarters anytime soon," he said. The look in his eyes made my hips shift again.

I could feel him hardening inside of me, and I quivered at the thought.

"We can't be slow this time, Quinn," he whispered before he kissed me deeply.

We were at headquarters within the hour. We moved rapidly, all things considered. Airik's wink made me blush as we walked through the doors. I was going to miss him. I wondered why they were calling us to the office at midnight.

Airik's Recorder, Miroll, met us as we walked into a room where the on-duty Recorders worked. They were all doing different things. All were wearing their earpieces, but they were either walking or curled up on the couch while talking to their Precogs.

"Airik, will you and Quinn come this way, please?" she said, leading us into a glass room.

"What's going on, Miroll?" Airik asked.

She hesitated. "We've never had this many details from either of you before. Your numbers were off the charts, double what you both usually get. And they came in simultaneously."

"Double?" Airik said, frowning. "That can't be right."

"This is the report," she said, scrolling through page after page of details.

"That's long, yeah, but there were two of us."

She cut him off.

"That's just yours, Airik. You've never done anything like this before. I would know. I've been your primary Recorder for over a decade."

"Why so long?" he said, glancing at me. "And how could they be simultaneous?"

"Nothing like this has happened before?" she asked, looking back and forth between us.

"Well," I said, looking at him. "There was that time when we found the apartment."

"That's right," he said, remembering.

"You've had simultaneous visions before?"

We both nodded.

"What was different about this vision? Did something change between this one and your normal Precogs?" she said. "We need to know if we can reproduce this level of detail.

Airik turned to look at me. I knew my face was turning bright red, and there was nothing I could do about it.

Miroll looked back and forth at us. "What is it?" she said.

"You know we're married, right?" Airik said.

"Yes, but what does that have to do with anything?" She broke off. "Oh."

Somebody had to say it what we were all thinking, so I did. "We had just finished making love, and we weren't separated yet," I said, feeling my face burning up with embarrassment. "The visions occurred before we could move apart."

"Really," she said, sounding fascinated.

"It's hardly reproducible unless the Precogs involved are married or dating," Airik said drily.

"It's good to know. You'll have to make a full report of the circumstances."

We both had our mouths open to object when Rob came running into the room, interrupting us.

"Thank goodness you're both here," Rob said, as he spotted us. "Come on. We're having a meeting in the main boardroom."

Airik and I looked at each other, shrugged, and followed him. When we entered the room, everyone was looking at a wall that followed all the Precog events happening in our Division. The wall made it easy for upper management to keep records of who was having visions at a particular time. There were a few other higher-ups in the room. In fact, it seemed that all the senior staff was here.

"We have a situation," Rob said.

"I'd say so," Airik said, monitoring the board. "I've never seen this many Precogs at once."

At the moment, the room looked like Christmas. Every light on the wall blinked furiously.

"Holy shit," I said under my breath.

"There's no way we can handle this volume," someone said. "We have to call all the Recorders we have, active or inactive. They need to answer from wherever they are. Even if everyone responds, we still won't have enough people."

"I'm on it," Rob said. "I'll send a message to every Recorder."

"What the hell is going on?" Airik said, looking around at his colleagues.

"It's a mass Precog, Airik," a short woman said.

"What does that mean?" I asked, speaking for the first time.

"It means that the Precog will affect a large number of people."

"You mean, like a virus that will start an epidemic, causing untold numbers of deaths all over the planet?"

"You had the same Precog, didn't you?" Airik said, looking at me.

Rob shook his head as he finished sending his message.

"Everyone's having the same Precog, Airik." He looked around at everyone in the room. "Look at the numbers from the other divisions. We're having a planet-wide emergency. Get the President on the phone. I need to talk to her right away."

CHAPTER 14

QUINN

"Rob should take you, Airik. He's not making sense."

"He says you're more versatile than I am. You have unique abilities, and they need me here."

I shook my head. "I won't do it. I won't take your spot."

He smiled warmly at me, then kissed me on the forehead. When he touched me, he accidentally brushed my third eye.

A vision of us in the snow passed through my mind and I slowed it briefly, knowing time was critical.

Airik, looking down at me. Airik crying. Our arms wrapped around each other, holding on for dear life. Me being unbelievably happy.

I didn't bother getting a timeline on it, because what I saw was unbelievable. "That's one of the inaccurate predictions," I said, pulling away from him.

He studied me as if he didn't recognize me. I couldn't stand it. He looked like he was trying to figure something out. "You'll go," he said. "Because they need you, not me."

"Airik, it's not right."

"It doesn't matter what's right and what's wrong. They want you." He kissed me. "I know you'll do great," he said.

I scowled as he walked out of the room. It would be a lot easier to leave him if he wasn't so nice about everything. And, of course, if I didn't love him so much.

Rob was assembling a ground team to go out and save the child. Based on all the other Precogs that had come in, they had written down every last detail of the group vision.

The girl and her mother were off-worlders and had recently come to Koccoran. They were unwittingly carrying a virus they had picked up somewhere on their interstellar travels. The virus could not transfer itself until the host died.

In the future, she dies, and her mother dies. The nurse brings their bodies back to the hospital, unknowingly contaminating herself. She gives it to other people at the hospital who are unable to fight it off and die as well. After their funerals, the number of people who have come into contact with the virus starts growing exponentially. By the time the virus is under control, Koccoran loses nearly thirty percent of its population. Most of the people who die are of childbearing age.

The virus was going to wipe out an entire race. The Koccorans weren't likely to survive this blow on top of all their other population issues. I felt desperate at the thought. They were only my adopted people, but my life here would disappear along with their inhabitants. The future looked bleak. There was little doubt of our accuracy with over a thousand visions corroborating the same story.

I strolled across the big Recorder room and into the boardroom where the rest of Rob's team had gathered. I felt like a fraud because I was a new graduate. Everyone else on the team had plenty of experience and training. But if Rob wanted me as part of his group, I wasn't about to say no. It would be the chance of a lifetime. I hadn't done any field work yet, but I hoped it would come quickly to me.

It felt terrible for me to take Airik's place like this. It seemed as if I was bumping him out. If I weren't here, he would be on this mission, and I couldn't help but feel guilty about it.

I didn't know anyone on the team, so I sat down at the table and waited. Rob wasn't only an instructor for the Institute and ground crew leader. He was also in charge of the entire Division of ground teams. He liked to keep his head in the field by doing missions as well as being in charge. I liked that about him. It meant he still knew what it was like on the front lines.

He smiled at me. "Good to see you here, Quinn."

"I couldn't turn down your offer," I said truthfully. I hoped the others wouldn't be annoyed by a green cadet and off-worlder coming along on such an important mission. I looked around. There were five people on the team: me, a male named Bral, a woman named Deerva, another woman that I didn't know, and Rob.

"The plan is simple, team," he said, leaning over and putting his palms down on the table. "We hike to the cabin before the child gets too sick. We give her an injection that will kill the virus, and we make sure she doesn't die. No problem."

We all chuckled. It sounded easy when he put it that way.

"We will have no communications on the mountain. It seems that the woman had a one-time use emergency communications unit she used to inform us about her problem. You've all seen the vision or read the report. She lives in a simple log cabin without electricity or water. She may come from Dantin or another no-tech planet to be content with her lifestyle."

We all smiled again. You would have to be from a planet like that to live without any technology. Yikes.

"We'll meet in twenty minutes to get outfitted for the hike. There's a blizzard coming in, people. Hopefully, we can make it up the mountain before the storm hits."

We glanced at each other. His dream seemed unlikely. I might not have been on Koccoran long, but I knew the chances of beating a blizzard were slim to none.

"Say your goodbyes. I'll see you in building A2 in twenty minutes," he said, wrapping up the meeting.

I went to find Airik. He was in his office, and I knocked on the door. His Recorder smiled at me on her way out.

"I'm heading out. I have to be ready to go soon," I said.

Airik walked over to me. "Good luck, Quinn. I'm sure you won't need it."

I felt my nerves overcoming me, and I looked up at him. I was worried. "There's a blizzard coming in, Airik. I might need more luck than you think."

"This is your second winter on Koccoran. You're not that fragile flower who wilted when the wind hit her face for the first time." He touched my cheek, and I closed my eyes.

"I guess not," I said. "I want to say goodbye, okay, Airik? I don't want to draw this out."

I reached my hand up around his neck and pulled him down to me. Then I kissed him, feeling all the love in my heart until we were both panting as we pulled away.

He looked at me as if he didn't understand something, but I had no time to decipher his facial expressions.

"Good..."

"Don't say good-bye," he said, putting his finger to my lips.

"Long life," I said and turned to leave.

"Quinn," he called after me as I went out the door.

"Yeah?" I said. I didn't look back.

"For what it's worth, I'm sorry I can't feel the way you want me to feel."

203

"I'm sorry too," I said.

I squared my shoulders. I would forget about Airik and how he didn't love me, and focus on this mission. It was important that I get it right. The entire planet was depending on us, and my life was going to be all about my career.

My other option, the love of my life, didn't love me at all.

AIRIK

I watched Quinn walk down the hall and had a strange feeling this would be the last time I saw her. Everything was going to be fine. She was going to be all right.

Then a full-on vision hit me so hard I couldn't speak to activate my computer. I was in the woods watching a tree fall on Quinn and me. The vision flashed to a casket with Quinn in it. She looked even whiter than when she was alive. She was dead.

My heart nearly stopped as I watched the brief vision flash through my mind. I couldn't lose her. It would be bad enough if she left me. I would be able to see her occasionally. But death? I could not imagine losing her to death.

"I don't love her," I said out loud. My voice lacked conviction.

I could be wrong about this Precog. I had to trust that the team would take care of her. I paced back and forth in my office, not understanding why I was anxious.

We were *alone* in my vision. Somehow we would get separated from the team. They wouldn't be able to protect her anymore. What if I was the only one who had this vision? What if I was the only one who could prevent her death?

If I were there when she died, surely I could prevent it.

Immediately the thought came to stop the team from leaving and tell them what I had seen. I walked as fast as I could to A2, one of the buildings set up for preparing field operations. It had every piece of equipment you might need and all the gear to carry it. I didn't think they could have left already.

When I arrived, there was no snowcopter, but I could see marks left in the snow left. A man was hanging around, closing things down.

"Did Operation Mountain Top leave yet?" I asked.

"That's classified, buddy."

I stepped closer so he could see who I was.

"Sorry, sir. They left about four minutes ago. They have good weather for flying, considering that there's a blizzard coming. They're going to drop them as far up the mountain as they can go in the storm. They'll have to make the rest of the trek on foot."

"Thanks." He nodded, going back to his work.

I felt my worry and desperation growing by the minute. Why hadn't I run all the way here? Why hadn't I insisted that I go instead of Quinn?

A plan crystallized in my mind. I would go after them. I would find her and save her. I would do an intervention by myself. The higher-ups frowned upon solitary engagements, but I didn't care. If I saved her, it would appease my conscience. When I told myself I was doing this was because it was the right thing to do, I could almost believe it.

When I was alone, I started outfitting myself for the hike. There was special clothing to wear if we expected prolonged exposure to the elements - a parka, thicker snow pants than the usual ones, a wool hat, and mitts. Quickly, I grabbed some other survival gear, and I was ready to go. I left a message for my superior for tomorrow's delivery. I grabbed snowshoes in my size and pulled on my backpack, doing up the buckles across my chest and hips.

The snowshoes looked like big tennis rackets, and I soon had them strapped to my feet. They would allow me to move much more quickly over snow without sinking in. I took off in a wide-legged run, moving as fast as I dared in the dusk and falling snow. The visibility was terrible, and I couldn't move quickly. A fallen tree could appear at any time. I had to remain alert.

I intended to take a short cut. I would head cross-country to a point farther up the mountain from the snowcopter landing zone. I hoped I would be able to catch them.

QUINN

The snowcopter had dropped us off as high up the mountain as it could safely fly, but it wasn't far enough. There was still a long, cold walk ahead of us if we wanted to reach the cabin. I wished Airik was with us. I hadn't been away from him for more than a day since our marriage.

It's not like we were joined at the hip or anything, but he was always around at home or work. Maybe I had gotten used to him. I grimly realized that I needed to get unused to him quickly. Soon we would be getting divorced, and I wouldn't see him again.

The thought was troubling but necessary. I couldn't live this half-life anymore. It was painful. Airik didn't love me, and he never would. That was my reality.

There was shouting up ahead. In front of me, people were crowded around one of the women from the team. I hadn't caught her name yet.

"What's wrong?" Rob said.

"It's a sprained ankle, I think. There was a fallen log under the snow, and I didn't see it. I twisted it when I fell."

"Can you still walk?" he said.

"Sorry, Rob. No way."

"No problem," he said. He motioned towards two men. "Make a travois and put her on it. You'll have to pull her back down the mountain, Bral."

"I can do that, sir," he said.

"Good. Deerva, rejoin us when they leave."

The other woman nodded and went to cut branches.

The rest of us continued up the mountain, feeling a little more nervous. Our party was already two people fewer, and we had barely started the journey. I wondered who would be next.

CHAPTER 15

AIRIK

I had misjudged my timing, but soon I could see the team ahead of me up the mountain. They were only about an hour ahead of me, and I had a visual on them. I was sure I could catch them.

The woman and her daughter couldn't possibly live past the tree line, so we were near the cabin. I needed to reach Quinn before she entered the forest.

I alternated between jogging and walking until I finally caught up with them. I got some strange looks as I raced past the bulk of the party. I was on my way to the front of the pack, where Rob and Quinn hiked side by side. It hurt to see them close together. Quinn appeared animated, and Rob listened to her as they walked. They looked the way I wanted Quinn and me to appear. They could be friends. Or perhaps more than friends.

When I reached them, I said, "Hi guys."

They gave me the same looks of surprise and consternation. I smiled at Quinn and kissed her on the cheek.

"What are you doing here?" Rob said, frowning. "You're supposed to be holding down the fort back at Headquarters."

"Can I talk to you alone for a minute, Rob?" I said.

210

"Sure. Do you mind, Quinn?"

She said, "No problem!" but she looked angry. There was no way around it. I wasn't going to tell her the real reason I was here. When a person knows something terrible will happen to them, their knowledge makes it harder to protect them. The first rule of intervention was to prevent the target from knowing about their death.

Once Quinn had dropped back far enough to be out of earshot, I told him. "I couldn't stay at Headquarters. I had a Precog."

"A Precog about what?"

"About Quinn, Rob. I saw her death. I think you have your hands full. I should worry about intervening on my own because you are busy saving the planet."

"No way, Airik. I won't condone it. We don't have many rules aside from 'make sure the target doesn't know about their imminent death', but 'never do an intervention by yourself' is up there. Too many things could go wrong."

"How about this," I said. "What if I take her back home? That way a tree can't fall on her. Easy, right?"

"You can't do that. What if I need a reading on the situation? She can call a vision like nobody's business." He paused. "She's even better than you."

"I know, Rob, but..."

"No buts, Airik. We're on my mission, and I say she stays. The intervention has to happen as we proceed. It's significant and the team needs her."

"Is the mission more important than Quinn's life?"

"We're talking about saving the lives of millions, Airik. Of course it's more important than one life."

I stared at him. As people who could stop death, we often got into philosophical debates about the job. But somehow the one-life-lost-is-worth-it-if-more-lives-are-saved argument wasn't working for me today.

Not if the life was Quinn's.

I glanced down and saw her smiling. She was talking to another team member. Proceeding with the mission would make it harder to prevent her death, but not impossible. I would not allow her life to be snuffed out.

"Fine. But I stay with her the whole time. And you must let me have the final word concerning the intervention."

"Whatever you want," Rob said. He was irritated as I was. "You're pretty concerned about this girl for a guy who doesn't love her."

"She's my wife. I have to take care of her. Saving her life is part of my job."

"You bastard. She needs more than someone to take care of her. You don't even know what you have, do you? What a waste."

"What's a waste?" I said, pulling his shoulder to make him look at me.

"The fact that she loves you. She wastes her feelings on you." He shook his head bitterly and kept walking.

"What would you know about it?" I said, jogging to catch up with him.

"She told me everything," he said. I glared at him, and he shrugged. "I guess Quinn needed a friend. She was emotional."

"She told you she loves me? She said those words?" I heard her say it in English last night, but I couldn't believe she would have told Rob something personal about herself.

"Yes," he muttered. His eyes looked resentful when he glanced at me. "She said you don't love her, and she knows it. She thinks she can't avoid it because people don't have control over who they love."

I didn't say anything.

"You're a fool, Airik."

"A fool?" I repeated. His words stung. People had called me a lot of things in my life, but I had never been called a fool.

"Yes, a fool. You just won't admit it until you lose her."

"Admit what, Rob? What do you mean?"

213

"How you feel about her. I've known you a long time, Airik."

I nodded. We had been friends since we were toddlers.

"And I have never seen you this worked up, confused, and desperate to save a target. You're a mess. You have been since the day you were married. Doesn't that tell you anything?"

"What are you getting at, Rob?"

"Do you even remember the feeling of loving a woman? Because if you don't remember, how do you know if you love Quinn?"

The thought was new to me. Did I remember what it felt like to love someone? I had not let myself love someone romantically for years. His question bounced around in my head and tormented me.

"Think about it," he said, a sour look on his face. "It will only take Quinn ten minutes to do a memory pull."

"What are you suggesting I do, Rob? Tell me straight."

"Get her to pull your memory of Gina. Remember? The girl who nearly made you killed yourself?"

I frowned. I hadn't remembered I had been suicidal over her for a long time.

"Once you remember what it feels like to love someone, then you can decide if you love Quinn or not. And whether the divorce is a good idea. You can decide if you want to win her back."

I had to change the subject. "You have feelings for her, don't you?"

"I do, Airik. So what? She's a beautiful person. But you're my best friend. She works for me. That's enough. I would never go there with her, Airik. You must know that."

I trusted Rob as much as my family. "I know."

"You should know this too. If you get divorced because you're stupid enough to let her go, then all bets are off."

I stared at him, mouth open, remembering the Precog Quinn had mentioned to me earlier. The one where she had seen her future self making love to Rob.

"Think about it, Airik."

I watched his back as he walked away from me. Quinn was putting a strain on our friendship. I wondered if the damage would be irreparable or if he and I would be able to get past her.

As I hiked, I tried to stop thinking about the questions he raised, but they kept coming back to my mind like wasps in summer.

The weather, at least, wasn't too bad for the first hour. It was snowing, but the wind was mild. The mood was peaceful and almost quiet.

When evening approached, Rob called a halt. We needed to make camp for the night. It was too dark to proceed. Hopefully, we would go the rest of the way tomorrow.

We quickly pitched our tents, made fires, and cooked dinner together. Afterward, we all helped clean up and sat around a fire drinking and trading intervention stories. Quinn avoided me and wouldn't meet my eye. She didn't refuse to share a tent with me. I had to take what I could get.

Later that night, I lay beside Quinn in our tent. We had zipped our bags together so that we had a double sleeping bag.

"I'm only using you for your body heat," Quinn said as she snuggled up to me. "Don't even think about getting lucky tonight, Airik."

"I wouldn't dream of it," I said. "I had another idea."

I could hear curiosity in her voice when she spoke.

"What is it?"

"I was wondering if you would do a memory pull on me." When she didn't answer, I wondered if she was passively refusing me.

"Which memory?" she said cautiously.

"When Gina broke my heart, I was suicidal afterwards. Can you blame me for wanting to bury it as deep as I could in my subconscious? I never want to feel that way again?"

"I don't blame you, Airik. But you know how a memory pull works, don't you? You'll have to experience the whole thing over again."

"I know." My stomach felt queasy at the thought, but Rob was correct. It was time for me to rediscover my heart and stop protecting myself. The barriers I had erected inside myself to keep out bad things were also keeping out good things.

I knew that, but the thought of what the memory pull would do to me made me want to vomit.

"Reliving the memory will be how you release it. If you accept it fully and experience it, then let it go, you will be free of the trauma forever."

"I understand, Quinn. I've been doing this a lot longer than you." The comment sounded snarky even to my ears. She made a frustrated sound. "I'm sorry. I didn't mean that."

"Shut up, Airik," she said, her voice harder than I had ever heard it before. "If you want to do this, I'm in charge. You do as I say."

I felt resistance rising inside me. I didn't want her to be in charge. I was always the one in control. Maybe I shouldn't do this if it meant I would have to relinquish power.

"If you can't give me the control in this situation, Airik, how are you going to relax enough for me to pull a memory?" It was like she had read my mind. "It won't work." She sounded disappointed.

I took a deep breath. "You're in charge, Quinn. Just tell me what to do." There was a wrenching inside me when I said the words, but afterwards came a sudden feeling of relief. I relaxed as she took my hand.

"Once I've identified the memory, I'll give you a preview. Please confirm that it's the correct memory. After I have your confirmation, I will pull it. My actions will cause your memory to replay in vivid detail in your mind as if you were there again."

"Yes, I understand."

"Do you agree to this memory pull?" It was a traditional ritual to get explicit verbal confirmation from the subject.

"I agree," I said.

"Here we go."

AIRIK, TWENTY YEARS AGO

"Hi, Gina," I said, walking up to a gorgeous brunette standing at her locker.

"Hey." Was it my imagination, or did she sound bored when she greeted me today? She seemed different from when we started going out at the beginning of the year. Her eyes used to light up when she saw me. Her reaction worried me, but the present I had for her would fix everything. "What's up?"

"I was wondering if you wanted to skip school." I leaned forward and whispered in her ear. "I have an exciting date planned."

She looked at me with interest. "*You*? You want to skip school? Weren't you telling me to focus? This is our last year, you want to get into the Institute, I want to get into college, we have to work hard...blah, blah, blah."

"I meant every word, Gina. My parents would kill me if they knew I was skipping. I want today to be about us, not school. I have a present for you. Will you come?"

She smiled at me. It was a genuine smile, like the ones she used to give me.

"Okay."

It was the beginning of summer. We hiked up into the mountains until we found our particular spot. It was the place where we'd first had sex. It had been the first time

219

for both of us, and I remembered the night being magical.

When we got to our spot, she looked at me. Her eyes were sensual.

"I don't know what your present is, but can I give you one first?" she asked. She pulled off her shirt and bra to display her perfect round breasts. She shimmied out of her clothing and sauntered up to me completely naked.

I was an eighteen-year-old boy. She was an eighteen-year-old girl with a perfect body. Was I going to say no? I felt time speed up as if someone had put my life on fast forward. I realized I was in my mind. Quinn must be speeding up my memory through the sex part. I didn't blame her.

All of a sudden, Gina and I lay side by side in the warm grass. We were naked as the day we were born. I quickly forgot this was just a memory.

"You know what, Airik? Whatever you may or may not be as a boyfriend, you are the most amazing lover I've ever had."

I smiled, basking in the compliment until I realized what had gone unsaid. My smile disappeared.

"Wait a minute. I thought you said I was your first? You've been with another guy?"

Gina's face fell as she realized what she had inadvertently revealed. "Guys," she said, not meeting my eye.

"Why did you lie to me? I wouldn't have cared."

"Because you thought I was a virgin. I didn't want to tell you I had already slept with three other guys. I didn't want you to believe I was a slut."

I did believe she was a slut *now*. But I wouldn't say it, and it didn't change the way I felt about her. Then I realized what she said about my suitability as a boyfriend. "Are you unhappy?"

"Airik. Of course I'm not happy."

"Why?" I asked. I felt the world spinning around me.

"Because you're boring. You always want to go to school. You try to control me, and you only like certain parts of me. I don't feel like I can be myself when I'm around you. It's too hard to live like that."

"You think I'm trying to control you?"

"I don't think, I know. I lied about being a virgin, but you don't like my clothes either."

"I just want you to dress more like who you are, so your exterior matches your interior."

"And not like a good-for-nothing girl without mental abilities."

"You're not good-for-nothing."

"You've never been to my house, Airik. Don't try to deny it. You think you're better than me. I knew it when we

221

started dating, but I thought your money would make up for your annoying, controlling personality."

She began to get dressed. "You know what? The sex almost did make up for everything else. Sex with you is mind-blowing. But it's not enough. I know you love me, Airik, but I don't love you. I can't go out with you any more."

I jumped up, pulling on my pants as she began walking down the mountainside.

"Gina, please. Can't we talk about this?" She couldn't be leaving me, could she?

"There's nothing to discuss, Airik. We've been over for months. I was just too scared to tell you."

"No," I said, my eyes full of tears. "Gina, I love you. Don't break up with me."

"Too late, Airik. We're already done. It's over."

I sank onto the grass, watching her until she was out of sight. The sun and the warm wind were an insult to my broken heart. Everything I had believed about Gina was a lie. I thought she had been a virgin, too. I thought she loved me. I thought she would someday marry me.

I pulled a key out of my pocket and stared at it. I had tied a red bow to the key. It symbolized all my hopes and dreams. I was about to give her this key as a present. It opened the door to an apartment I had rented for us for next year. We would live in it while I went to the Institute and she went to college.

I threw it as far as I could down the mountain and buried my head in my hands, tears running down my face. "I will never let another woman hurt me like this," I said out loud, through a haze of pain. I felt like my chest was being split open. "I will never love again. Because it hurts too fucking much."

CHAPTER 16

QUINN

Well, the memory certainly explained a lot. Airik was crying on my shoulder. He was lost in his mind.

I was crying, too. I had experienced everything with him, and it had been awful. I liked my first boyfriend. I hadn't loved him the way he had loved Gina. He gave her his heart and soul. It hadn't broken my heart when we decided to split up. I was upset, of course. But not like Airik.

He truly loved that girl.

The thought made me jealous. Why couldn't he love me like he loved her? Of course, I had seen the answer in his memory. Airik had sworn he would never love a woman again because it hurt too much.

Our relationship was in trouble. Sometimes people couldn't let go of a trauma because it became part of their character. Sometimes they didn't even want to give up the hurt because they became accustomed to the pain or numbness. They didn't know who they would be without it.

I couldn't see Airik releasing his pain because it made sense for him to grasp it tightly. His past trauma was protecting him from getting hurt again. I understood why he would want to feel protected.

His sleep was restless. I knew not to wake him. I wasn't sure why I had come out of the memory unless it was over already and we were in the aftermath. Either way, I should leave him alone.

I rose and looked out the flap of the tent. The sun was coming up already. We had been working all night, but I didn't feel tired. I felt sad. My heart was breaking. I now knew my love for Airik would always be unrequited. I had lost the brief flicker of hope that sprang into existence when he followed us. I didn't know why he had appeared, but it wasn't because he loved me and wanted to confess his feelings to me.

It was difficult in the tiny tent, but I quietly got dressed. I wrote a quick message telling him I had gone ahead. I would see him when the group caught up with me. We all had the same map. If I got lost, I could call a vision to tell me where to go. I didn't want to be next to Airik all day.

In fact, I wanted to get away from all of them. If I got a head start on my hike, they would be behind me. When I got to the cabin, I would wait until they caught up. We could do the intervention together. I would be okay. It wasn't even snowing anymore.

I crawled out of the tent. The camp was quiet. The rising sun made the horizon a brilliant pink as it rose into the cloudy sky. I drew in a lungful of cold air. My breath looked like smoke in the frigid temperatures. It was just like my vision of how my true love and I would die together.

I had tried to forget that vision, but now I allowed myself to think about it again. Maybe the vision was why Airik didn't love me. I was supposed to love and be loved by another.

The morning was beautiful. Maybe I would get used to this climate after all. The stillness of the dawn only seemed to happen on these freezing mornings. I smiled sadly. The planet was lovely.

When I looked back at the tent, my smile disappeared as I thought of my love. I squared my shoulders and gave a firm nod, striking out in the direction of the cabin.

AIRIK

I sat straight up in bed. Something was wrong.

Why were there tears covering my cheeks? I wiped my eyes. My memories came crashing back in waves thanks to the memory pull. Once more, I experienced Gina leaving me, and I relived how much it hurt. I let out a shuddering breath. I had been afraid to think about Gina since she left me. Now that I had faced my fear and pain, I felt different. My soul was lighter because of Quinn.

I looked around. I was alone. Where was she? Maybe she had gone to the bathroom. It was barely light. I lay down and waited for her to come back. But when she didn't return after a few minutes, I began to worry.

It occurred to me to check for her clothes. They were gone. Was she outside somewhere making breakfast? I dressed as quickly as I could and left the tent a disorganized mess. She couldn't be alone right now. I couldn't stop seeing my vision of her death.

Once you had a target in your sights, you didn't let them leave until you changed the possible future. If they left your side, you never knew what was going to happen. Sometimes your presence in their lives affected what was going to happen and made it impossible for you to protect them. That had happened to me once when I was a rookie. I swore I would never let it happen again.

Now my wife's life was on the line. I searched the camp but didn't see any sign of her. I went around the perimeter and found tracks leading off into the forest.

They were in the direction of the cabin. Had she left without even telling me?

I remembered that I forgot to check my messages when I realized she was missing. There wasn't a message from Quinn, but I found a scribbled note. I skimmed it. She had decided to go ahead without me. She said she wanted her space.

Normally that would be fine, except this time I knew she would die in the forest. I had to find her. I was almost out the door, completely unprepared and ready to follow her tracks before I realized I was an idiot. Five more minutes wouldn't make a difference. The extra time would let me get ready for anything I might meet in the woods.

I ran back to our tent and emptied my backpack, only leaving emergency supplies, a change of clothes for both of us, and a few extra pairs of socks. Then I sent a quick message to Rob, telling him what was happening. I strapped on my snowshoes and raced off, following her tracks. I knew I would have to run to catch up with her.

What if this was when my vision was becoming reality? What worried me the most was that things might have changed. Now she might be going to die alone. In an ideal world, I would take a fresh vision to recalibrate the future.

The thought gave me wings, and I moved quickly. I had to slow myself down to pace my movements. The last thing I wanted to do was hit a wall and be stuck, unable to move, while Quinn was still lost somewhere in the forest.

I followed beside her tracks, not over them. The holes she made struggling through the deep snow could make me tip and fall. My equipment was more useful on fresh snow than trampled snow.

By this time, the snow was falling so quickly I could hardly see. I wasn't going to let anything stop me from following the tracks. I tried to move faster. I knew the snow was coming down so hard it would soon cover her tracks. I would have no way of knowing which way she went.

The wind came up suddenly. I pulled my scarf up to my eyes and my hat down to my eyebrows. Leaving only my eyes exposed would keep my face from freezing. With the speed of the wind and the temperature right now, I knew a high wind chill made the weather seem colder. If I was back home, I imagined a warning would say: *Exposed skin will freeze in under a minute.*

When you heard that alert, you either stayed inside or made sure you were covered up. Since remaining indoors wasn't an option, I protected myself from the bitter cold and kept going.

When she saw me, she wasn't ready to talk. "Airik, leave me alone!"

"I wanted the memory pull to work, Quinn."

"But it didn't."

"Not for lack of trying," I pointed out.

"Forget it. I don't care. Why did you bother trying to find me out here?"

"I was worried about you," I said. In my mind, I saw the tree falling on us again. "Anything could happen."

She stepped backward with an expression of shock on her face. "You had a vision about me, didn't you? There's a particular look you get when you're doing an intervention on a target. Did you see my death?"

"Quinn, don't say silly things."

"You didn't say no." She frowned. "And you wouldn't tell me even if you did." She started muttering to herself.

"Quinn, please. Let's find everyone else."

Like magic, the remains of our party came into view. They were still far down the mountain but moving towards us at a fast clip. Rob was probably afraid we would go in without him and steal his glory. I wondered if my bitterness was coming out. He was probably worried about us. We watched as they approached. They caught up with us in a few minutes.

"Is this the place?" Rob asked.

"Do you know of any other cabin on this mountaintop at these coordinates?" I said sarcastically.

He gave me an angry look, and I couldn't help grinning. Rob went over the plan again. It was straightforward. We didn't anticipate any problems.

"Okay, people," he said. "Let's head out."

Quinn glanced at me. She moved ahead inconspicuously so she wouldn't have to walk beside me. My heart felt like it was breaking in two. I fell to the back of the group. That's why I didn't know what was happening when the shouting started.

Someone screamed, and everyone else gathered around a body. I ran to catch up and see what was going on. Deerva lay on the ground. She had a big burn mark on her ankle. It was visible through her partially burned snow pants. She groaned and shook; she seemed to be extreme pain. The injury looked bad enough to make me sick to my stomach. I turned away from the scene, trying to keep down my breakfast.

Rob barked out orders and quickly moved towards her to begin treatment. Soon her keening stopped, and he had the wound bandaged and wrapped up. He must have given her a painkiller. Otherwise, I'm sure she be unconscious with such a bad burn.

"What was that?" I exclaimed as quietly as possible.

"Tripwire. There's a laser perimeter around the house," he said. He shone a special light onto the area that showed the defensive mechanism.

"I can't believe they have any defenses, and I can't imagine why they would be set to burn us." I said. "Who are these people?"

"No one knows. We should proceed with extreme caution. I don't want any other team members getting hurt. Deerva needs to heal. Her burn is all the way to the bone on her shin."

"Rob. Shut up," I said. My stomach was doing a flip.

Quinn walked up to us and looked at me, then back to Rob. "What's the problem?"

"Airik is squeamish about physical injuries," he said to Quinn. He turned back to me. "You're turning green. Are you going to be okay?"

"I'll be fine when you stop describing it in such graphic detail," I said, clenching my teeth.

"What happened?" Quinn said.

"She set off a tripwire that's set to burn anyone who crosses it. It's homemade but deadly."

Quinn glanced at me, then murmured, "I was ahead of her. I decided to drop back and talk to you. Before I knew it, she was screaming. It should have been me."

I was shocked. "Quinn," I said, studying her face. She gazed back and reached up, cupping her hand to my cheek. She was a beautiful sight. What made me unable to love her?

Rob interrupted my thoughts. "The cabin is lit up now so we can see everything. Please proceed cautiously. The mission is more dangerous than we previously anticipated."

Everyone nodded. I stepped over, holding my breath. Quinn followed me carefully. Rob and Deerva came next. He supported her as she limped along. We avoided two other tripwires before we finally got close to the cabin.

We were moving slowly toward the door when it opened, and the nose of a gun peeked out.

"Get down," Rob yelled. We all dropped flat on the snow as several blasts shot by overhead. Deerva had rolled a few feet before she came to rest. She clumsily fell, hampered by her hurt leg.

Rob pulled out a gun, but no one else carried anything to defend ourselves. Bursts of gunfire went back and forth for several minutes before I heard Quinn shout "Stop shooting!" She stood and raised her hands in a gesture of surrender.

"Quinn, what are you doing?" I whispered.

"I know what's going to happen," she said. "It's okay."

I couldn't relax. She had opened herself to the future. She must have seen we would be safe if she stopped everyone from shooting.

She might not have realized that things could change. People made different choices all the time. Neither the future nor the present was predetermined. What we saw were possibilities, not certainties. I thought having Quinn approach a madwoman was a bad idea.

"Please stop shooting," she said. She hadn't moved and kept her hands up. "Someone is going to get hurt. It might be your daughter."

The gun disappeared. In its place appeared a face which peering out into the snowy day to see Quinn. She looked like an older woman, with a wrinkled face and eyes that squinted. Her hair was not combed. Her clothes looked ragged.

"Get out of here. All of you. I only want to talk with her," the woman said.

Rob looked at me. I shook my head.

"I have to leave a partner with her. We won't leave her by herself," Rob called out.

"Fine," she said. "One more."

Rob nodded to me. "Be safe." He stood up with Deerva. They moved as quickly as they could, limping back the way we had come. He would take her back to camp and get help to retrieve her. Someone would take her to the hospital.

"Would you turn off the tripwires, please?" Quinn said. "One of our people was already badly hurt."

A guilty look flashed across the woman's face, but it didn't last long. Within seconds, a stern expression was back. This would be harder than it seemed back at headquarters. She disappeared inside her cabin. After a moment, the lasers illuminated by Rob's device disappeared.

"Come in quickly," the woman said. "I need to reactivate the defense system."

Quinn marched toward the house. I scrambled to keep pace with her. The woman opened the door to let us in. Inside the cabin, the room was plain and bare. On one side of the room, a girl lay sleeping on a bed. On the other side was a kitchen with a wooden table and two benches.

"Please sit down," the woman said, indicating one of the benches.

"I'm Quinn," she said. "This is Airik."

I noticed she didn't introduce me as her husband.

"My name is Dorelle," the woman said. Now that I could get a better look at her, I thought she might be the same age as me. I gazed at the sick girl and hoped the rest of our mission would go as planned. I had never had one go this far off course.

"You're probably wondering why we've invaded your cabin," Quinn began.

"I know why you're here," Dorelle said, biting off the words.

Quinn and I blinked and glanced at each other, waiting for her to explain herself.

"We came here from Dantin. It is my home planet and where my daughter was born. It's a low technology world. If you know who to pay, the right people can sneak a coded message to a space station in orbit. You can get transported out if you're lucky. We don't use credits, but if you gift enough land, someone will help you get off-world.

"We knew that," Quinn said. "What we don't know is why you came here."

"It's because of my husband," she said. "He loved Dantin and never wanted to leave. But he got sick with a virus. I knew he was dying, so I paid to have us beamed to the space station. I thought they could save him."

Her eyes filled with tears. "He died anyway. The doctors couldn't do anything. They said it was too late for him. We couldn't go back because we had traded all our belongings to reach the doctor."

She took a deep breath and continued her story.

"I was healthy. I managed to get a job washing dishes on the space station while Golda went to school. Eventually, I had saved enough to buy passage on a spaceship. I knew where I wanted to emigrate."

"Koccoran?" I said.

She nodded. "We passed all the tests. They let us in based on my petition. We were refugees without a home. I discovered this cabin, and it wasn't expensive. Golda and I knew how to live off the land. We bought supplies and started a garden. We were doing fine."

"Until Golda got sick, too," Quinn said.

"That's right. The doctors performed a lot of medical tests on us, but they still missed it. I thought if they let us in, we were clean."

"But you carried a virus, and now Golda is sick," Quinn said. "Dorelle, this is bigger than a single sick child." Quinn stood up and approached her. "If we don't give her the antidote, there will be more sick children. There will be an epidemic. Many wives will lose their husbands." Her eyes cut over to me. "Parents will worry about their children's lives."

"I know," she said. She didn't look surprised at Quinn's revelations.

"How do you know?" I asked.

"Why do you think I chose Koccoran? I knew that they would be accepting of my gift."

"Which gift do you mean?"

Quinn already knew all about Dorelle's gift. "She's a Precog, just like us."

CHAPTER 17

AIRIK

I rolled my eyes. Of course she was. No wonder she had activated her defense system. She knew we were coming.

"If you just want a new life, why do you have all this weaponry?" I said.

She looked down at her hands. "I was afraid that we were still carriers even though we made it through customs. I foresaw a group of people coming and attacking us. That's when I installed the defense system. It took the last of my credits, but it was worth it."

"We didn't come to fight you," I said.

"Seems like I'm under attack right now," she said. When I thought about it, I had to admit that she was right. I would have thought we were attacking her, too.

"We have the antidote. Where is your daughter? We can save her."

"I'm sorry. I can't let you do that," Dorelle said, lifting her gun. She had never set it down. Now it was pointing straight at us.

"Why not?" Quinn said. "It will neutralize the virus and prevent it from spreading. If your daughter dies, the virus will infect everyone that has come within twenty feet of her. They'll quarantine us, but the epidemic will still happen."

I looked at her sharply. "How do you know that?"

"I had another vision on the way here," she explained.

"I couldn't tell."

"I know. I can have them without any interruption in my activities now." She looked at me like it was commonplace, but I don't think she fully understood how unusual it was. I had never heard of anyone who didn't go into a trance when having a vision.

"Koccoran already has population issues," she said to Dorelle. "If this virus is allowed to spread, it will wipe out many women of childbearing age. It will mean a death sentence for their entire race. Please think about what you're doing."

"I *am* thinking. I knew you were coming, and I read up on your antidote."

"How?" I said. "I thought you didn't have any technology here."

"I got a connection and the defense system. I got what I need," she said. "I can learn. Your cure could make her deaf or blind. Maybe both."

"The chances of that happening are less than 10 percent," I said.

"She's not your child. I'd rather she died. We'll be careful and burn her body."

"You want her to die?" Quinn said. "Are you crazy?"

239

"Where I come from, if you're deaf or blind, you might as well be dead. You can't take care of yourself."

"We've made advances since those days."

"Yeah, yeah. Technology. You all believe gadgets are wonderful. But it couldn't figure out we had that damn virus in our blood, could it? If it can't help with the most important things, what good is it?"

I didn't have an answer to that.

"Dorelle, look at all you've gone through to protect your daughter. You can't stop now. We're her best shot."

"You won't convince me. I won't have her live to be a cripple."

"What about Koccoran? They took you in when you had nowhere to go. Don't you owe them? How can you unleash an epidemic on an entire planet?" Quinn said.

The woman sniffed and rubbed her nose. "I have to take care of my own. I can't worry about an entire world."

"You can do both," Quinn said.

"Just because I can doesn't mean I will. You have to leave now," Dorelle said, gesturing with her gun towards the direction of the door.

Quinn's eyes flicked to mine and then to Golda, who was tossing and turning feverishly on the couch. I nodded my head.

"Sure," Quinn said. "We'll leave. But before we go, can we have a drink of water?"

Dorelle made a face but turned to the kitchen. Quinn tackled her in an instant. The woman fought back, punching and hitting Quinn. The gun went off. I ignored the fight and moved towards the girl.

I had my syringe out and pulled off the cap. I pulled off the bedcovers and slightly pushed up her nightdress, jabbing my needle into her thigh and injecting the contents into her body.

The little girl whined and started crying. I held it until I counted to twenty.

"It's done." I sat back and ran a medical scanner over her body to confirm the antidote had worked.

Just like that, we had saved the planet.

QUINN

The little girl's fever had broken already. Dorelle, although furious initially, wasn't upset any longer. She saw her daughter getting better every minute, and she didn't appear to have any lasting injuries.

I didn't have anything to do. Dark thoughts were starting to infect my mind again. I glanced at Airik. He was busy sterilizing the cabin with Rob, making sure they disinfected everything. He wouldn't even notice I was gone. I just needed some air. I would go for a walk, come back, and help with whatever else needed to be cleaned up.

The door was open. When I let myself out, I was glad to see there was only a mild snowfall. After a few minutes, I had my first misgivings. The snow was becoming thicker. I decided to turn around and go back. But when I turned to follow my tracks, I saw that they were already disappearing beneath the fresh powder.

I frowned. I had to get used to being on my own and doing my own thing. In a couple of weeks, we would be divorced, and I wouldn't be able to depend on him to save me. I was a grown woman now. It was time to pull up my big girl panties and take care of myself.

The cabin should be directly behind me, so I tried to turn around and go back the way I came. As I walked, the trees and brush became denser. Was I going in the right direction? I didn't remember all these obstacles on the way out. I had to fight my way through the vegetation several times. Occasionally I had to go all the way around some plants because there was no way through except on my stomach.

I tried to call a vision, but I was so scared that I couldn't activate one. There was too much stress. The adrenaline in my system would block my ability.

The forest suddenly didn't seem as friendly as it had seemed back at camp. I kept walking. Instead of getting brighter, the atmosphere seemed dark and oppressive. It worried me. I knew the trees would block out the light, but it felt like the sun was disappearing around me. Incredibly, the snow began to fall more and more thickly. Soon I could barely see anything more than a few feet in front of me.

Was I caught in a blizzard?

As soon as the thought crossed my mind, the wind picked up. It blew hard and wailed through the trees. I knew my walk had been a bad idea at this point, but there was nothing I could do but keep moving. There wouldn't be a shelter for me. There was no point in going back. I had to find the cabin.

An hour later, as I lifted my aching legs and took another step through the deep snow, I wasn't sure I would ever find the cabin. Who knew walking could be so difficult when there was a foot and a half of snow on the ground? I felt exhausted.

I wished that Airik was here, but I knew it was impossible for him to appear out of nowhere. He had been busy when I left. Who knew when he would notice I was gone? Even if he did, he would still have to find me.

I wondered if it made sense for me to sit down and take a nap. I was tired and could use the energy boost. I considered the idea for a minute, but then I remembered Airik telling me never to stop moving when you were out in the cold. I didn't want to fall asleep because I would freeze to death and never wake up.

But having a rest was tempting.

I kept walking and then I felt my boot catch on something I couldn't see. I pulled, but I was stuck. What was it? I started to dig through the snow. After a minute, I got down to the ground. The boot and my foot were caught under a root. I had managed to get myself wedged in tightly. I tried pulling myself out until I became sweaty and frustrated. I thought about slipping my foot out of the boot, but I couldn't even do that. I would have to wait for someone to find me.

The trees around me were enormous. It would take two people joining hands to encircle a trunk. The trees had been still all the times I had been out for picnics and hikes in the woods. Right now, the trees were whipping back and forth, the wind lashing them into a swift motion.

I was surprised at how afraid the trees made me feel. If one of them came crashing down, it would be incredibly dangerous. I had never been scared of trees before. The thought seemed ridiculous until I looked up at them again and saw the first one fall.

The wind moved it back and forth. There was a sickening crack and the sound of a massive object falling. The branches swished against the other trees. I watched it in fascination until I realized it was heading directly toward me. I tried to move and remembered my foot was caught.

I was going to die, and there was nothing I could do.

AIRIK

It took me a few minutes to notice that Quinn was gone. But when I did, I lost my mind. Rob had to calm me down.

"Rob, I have to find her immediately. I never got to do an intervention. The future must have changed when I came to her. She's out in the forest with a blizzard approaching."

"Airik, calm down." Rob said, putting his hands on my shoulders. "You can't help her if you're panicking."

I took a deep breath and nodded. "I'm going to get her. I'll stay calm. I promise."

"Take your snowshoes. It will be faster," he said.

I dressed and moved out the door in minutes. I attached the snowshoes to my boots and then I was running into the forest following a trail that was quickly disappearing. Soon I had to use my minimal tracking skills to follow her. Her trail was vanishing.

As I crossed a small clearing, I spotted her red coat ahead of me. I could barely see it through the falling snow. When the wind blew strongly, I could see a flash of red. I hoped she was still alive. The coat wasn't moving.

What was going on? I started to run, feeling the events of the vision drawing closer to the present.

When I approached her, I saw she was struggling and pulling on her right leg. She appeared to be stuck in the ground.

There was a cracking noise, and I looked up. One of the giant trees had broken and was coming down. As my eyes projected its trajectory, I knew this was the moment. It was going to fall on her unless I stopped it.

Time seemed to slow down for me. She was no longer pulling on her boot and looked up as the huge tree fell towards her. It caught on another tree and stopped falling. I reached her at the same time.

"Quinn," I yelled. "Come on."

"My foot's stuck. Get out of here," she said, her face afraid and desperate. "We don't have to die together."

That was when I realized I loved her.

I felt something snap inside me. The feelings I had trapped behind my walls and refused to acknowledge came rushing out. I smiled at her, then glanced up at the tree precariously balanced on a tiny branch of another tree.

I took her hands and leaned toward her. I knew my life was about to end. It didn't matter. Before I died, I would have the chance to tell her.

"Yes, Quinn. We do both have to die. I love you, and I can't live without you."

"What?" she said, not believing what I was saying.

"I love you," I said again. I leaned in and kissed her.

When the tree hit us, it was over quickly. I barely felt a thing.

CHAPTER 18

QUINN

I was dead. There was no other explanation. A moment ago there had been an enormous tree falling on us. It was just like in my vision, except I hadn't known Airik would be next to me. Now I felt nothing. No pain. Nothing could have stopped the tree from crushing us.

Then I heard Airik's voice.

"Quinn?"

Good. He was with me. I hoped we were in heaven and not hell together. I thought I had been a good person, and he was too. Hopefully, we were going to be together for eternity.

I suddenly remembered what he said before we died. I had said we didn't both have to die.

He said he loved me.

I didn't know what had happened. Maybe the memory pull had worked or perhaps it was the threat of imminent death. Both had a way of brushing away unimportant things in life and allowing people to focus on crucial details. Either one could help a person let go of everything that wasn't serving them and enable them to see the truth.

Unfortunately, it was too late for us. Would we still love each other in the afterlife? What if we were being reincarnated instead of going to heaven? I would have to find him once more. How would I know him in another body? Would I have to go through the pain of finding him again?

Damn. I didn't want to be dead anymore.

"Quinn," Airik's voice was more insistent now. "I need you."

That couldn't be Airik. The voice sounded desperate and belonged to a person who wanted me. Could it be him?

"Please wake up," he said, his voice pleading. I felt him shaking my body. Maybe we weren't dead. But how could that be? "Open those blue eyes one more time and tell me you're okay. I will never take you for granted again."

I focused on my eyes and managed to flutter them open.

"Quinn," he gasped. I felt him covering my face with kisses. "I thought you left me."

I looked up. Snow was falling on me and melting on my face.

"How are we alive?" I asked, gazing up at him.

"Quinn, please listen to me. I can't wait another second to tell you." He carefully shaped his lips and spoke in English. "I love you."

I stared at him in amazement.

"What? Did I say it wrong? I didn't say your cat has green socks or something, did I?" he asked, reverting to Standard.

"No. It was perfect. How do you know those words?"

"Let's just say there was a girl who inspired me to learn her language. Maybe you can teach me some more."

"Do you mean it?"

"I have never meant anything more in my life. I now realize that what I felt for Gina was nothing compared to what I feel for you. You are the one I love, Quinn. Like I said, I can't live without you."

"I love you, too, Airik." I frowned, looking around. We appeared to be in a cave, but it was open to the sky. "How did we escape being crushed by the tree?"

"We didn't," he said, reaching out and touching the wall of the cave. His finger came back covered with a substance as black as charcoal.

"What is that?"

"You did it, Quinn. You were almost on fire. You generated so much heat that when the tree hit us, you burned through it."

"I couldn't have done that on my own, Airik. It was like our shared vision. Remember how we amplified each other's abilities? That must have happened again. Instead of being fueled by anger, it was powered by love, which must be more powerful. You gave me the strength to burn through this huge tree."

It seemed impossible, yet here we were.

"Quinn," he said, his eyes full of longing. "Will you forgive me for being a hopeless jerk who couldn't see what he had right in front of him?"

I smiled. "Of course I will, Airik. Now, kiss me like you love me."

He gave me a sexy grin. "That shouldn't be a problem..." he said, his eyes warming. "...because I do."

His lips were on me, and I thought I was in heaven. I had never imagined I could feel this good on any planet.

"So just like that, you guys neutralized an enormous threat to our civilization?" Neesa said. She looked impressed.

"I guess so," I said. "The people back at headquarters said as soon as our intervention was complete hundreds of Precogs started coming in again."

"This time, the visions were of our population numbers going up. Birth rates will be on the rise again," Airik explained.

"It was pretty good for my first intervention," I said, allowing myself to smile a bit.

"Pretty good?" Airik said, gazing at me with an adoring look on his face. "Rob and I have been on plenty of missions between us. The use of your skills, your presence of mind with Dorelle, and your courage were equivalent to experienced ground team members. You're one of us now."

"I'm not sure I trust your assessment of her skills," Neesa said.

Airik got an exasperated look on his face. "Why not?"

"I don't think you'd be able to give an unbiased opinion. You're obviously in love with her."

My heart warmed, and Neesa smiled at me. Airik walked over to Neesa. He reached out and deliberately messed up her hair.

"Hey," she said, trying to finger comb it back in place. "We're not kids anymore. You can't do things like that to me."

"I can and I will. If you're going to bug me, then I can bug you."

"You're acting like you don't like it, Airik, but I know you do. You want everyone to notice how you're head-over-heels for her."

He shrugged and sat back down beside me on the couch, draping his arm carelessly over my shoulders. Now I could tell he was trying to look nonchalant. Every movement, every look, and every word since the intervention had a subtext and it was always the same. It always said *I love you.*

I could feel it in his gaze, in the way he touched me, and in the tone of his voice. I had never been happier. Neesa was right. We were a cute couple — maybe even sickening to those who had to watch us.

"You've been moved up from junior Precog to full Precog, Quinn?" Neesa asked from the kitchen where she was making a salad for supper.

"Yes. I'll be doing some work in the office and also going out with ground teams where my particular skills can be useful."

"And they'll be using us as a team of Precogs, as well."

"Because you can amplifying each other's powers. If you're touching Quinn, is your empathic ability stronger?"

"Yes. By the way, green isn't a good color for you, Neesa," Airik commented.

Was Neesa envious of us?

"I'm not jealous. Not really," she said quickly.

Airik stared at her until she relented.

"Maybe I am a little. You guys are happy now, and I wish I were too."

"I'm sure you're going to find someone soon," Airik said. His tone of voice made Neesa glance at him sharply.

"How sure are you?" she said. "Have you had a vision about me?"

"Neesa…" he said, holding up his hands and shaking his head.

"Tell me," she said, coming over to the couch and waving salad tongs at him. "Tell. Me."

"No. You'll see when it happens."

"You can't get anything out of him when he has his mind made up. I guess I'll have to wait," she said, going back to the kitchen with a little more bounce in her step.

"Did you really have a vision?" I whispered.

"You'll have to wait and see, too," he said infuriatingly.

I huffed. "Fine."

"Your anniversary's coming up," Neesa said. "What are you going to do?"

"I have a surprise planned for Quinn," Airik said. "We're going to have a romantic dinner."

"I hope it's after the dinner Mom's planned. She'll kill you if you don't let us celebrate it with the entire family."

"The whole family?" I said, remembering all the people who had been at the wedding. I still didn't remember every name.

"Just the immediate family," Neesa corrected herself.

"Oh, sure. That's fine," I said. There were enough brothers and sisters and their offspring to keep me frantically remembering names. As long as it wasn't the extended family too, I thought I could handle it.

"Don't worry, sis. I'll take care of you," Neesa said. She winked at me. "I got your back."

AIRIK

I checked to make sure everything was perfect and then waited for Quinn to come home. When she finally walked through the door, I jumped up and went to her.

"Surprise," I said, helping her take off her coat. "Why are you late? I was expecting you an hour ago."

"I had an errand to run."

"Are you ready for our private anniversary celebration? Yesterday's dinner at Mom and Dad's was for everyone else. Tonight is for us."

"Oh," Quinn said, and she flashed a beautiful smile at me. Her bright blue eyes twinkled. "It smells good in here."

"I made dinner."

"Sounds great," she said and followed me into the dining room.

After we finished eating, we moved to the living room and sat on the couch. "I have something for you, Quinn," I said. "It's not a traditional anniversary present, but I hope you'll like it."

I held a package out to her. She took it carefully.

"What is it?" she asked.

I gave her a look that said, as-if-I'd-tell-you.

"Open it."

She tore open the box and looked at me in confusion.

"Are these my wedding rings? Why are you giving them back to me?"

I had asked her to give them to me. I told her I would have them cleaned, buffed, and shined. I did all that and something extra. "Look inside," I said.

She picked them both up and rotated them in the light so she could read the engraving.

"Stronger. Together," she read. "Wow. That's beautiful, Airik."

Her eyes filled with tears, and I wondered if the writing had been a good idea. I wanted to explain myself.

"It was supposed to symbolize how we can augment our powers when we're together, and how you and I make each other stronger when we're a couple." I scratched my head, feeling foolish. "I thought it would be romantic. We can have them engraved with something else if you like."

She cut me off with a kiss. When she finally pulled back, I gave her a smile.

"I love them. They're amazing. Now I have two presents for you," she said, handing me a similar box.

When I opened it, I saw my wedding rings, which I hadn't been wearing for the past week. My hands got so dry in the winter that I couldn't stand anything touching my skin.

"You took my rings?"

"I might have gotten them engraved, too."

We laughed.

"Great minds think alike," I said.

"Fools seldom differ," she finished. "We both know I am a fool for you, Airik. Just read them, okay?"

I squinted, turning the rings to make out the words. It took me a minute to realize they weren't written in Standard, but English.

"I love you," I read, pronouncing the foreign words slowly, trying to pronounce them correctly.

"How about the other one?" she said.

"Saransho belava," I said.

"That's 'I love you' in your language, right? It doesn't say your cat has green socks or something?" I joked, repeating his words back to him.

"It is," I said, tears coming to my eyes. I quickly blinked them back but not before she saw them.

"Do you like them? Or should I have gotten you a gift card?"

"I love them," I said. "It's thoughtful."

"So were yours," she said.

"Do you know what I have next on the schedule?"

"I can guess," she said, starting to unbutton her blouse.

"You read my mind."

"Maybe I had a vision," she said, capturing my lips and kissing me.

We had been together for one year, but I knew — even without a vision — it was only the beginning.

CHAPTER 19

QUINN

"Come here, sweetie. Daddy's trying to do some work. You and I didn't finish the puzzle," I said, scooping up my daughter and swinging her around until she squealed. She loved being with Airik. Whenever he tried to get some work done at home, Lalla always was stuck to him like glue. She didn't like separation from her father, but she would come with me because she loved puzzles.

"Wait, Quinn," he said, his eyes still on his screen. "I just got the results of the intervention you foresaw. The one you didn't tell me about because it happened before I knew you were a Precog. The little girl got hit by a car, remember?"

I looked at the ground silently. I couldn't stare at him.

"Don't worry. We saved her. The Precogs on the scene are foreseeing a long life for her. She will be an old woman someday."

"Really?" I asked, relief filling my chest. "Thank you so much for telling me, Airik." He winked at me, and I smiled back. I carried Lalla out of Airik's office and felt as light as air.

"One more thing, Quinn." I turned to him. "Rob and Deerva have invited us over for dinner next week."

"Sounds great." After their adventure together, Rob and Deerva started dating almost immediately. They recently moved in together. No one was happier for them than I was. Especially since it meant that Rob wasn't interested in me anymore.

Airik and I had been together for three years. Lalla was fifteen months old. I thought we conceived her on our first anniversary, but I didn't have any proof.

Everyone else had been shocked that we quickly got pregnant, but it didn't surprise me. They thought it was because I was human. I knew we would have a big family like Airik's. I never had any family except my father. It pleased me more than anyone knew to have many people around who loved us and loved my daughter.

It made me happy to see her with all her cousins, aunts, and uncles. Her Nana and Papa were over almost every day. Their place was like her second home. She loved them all.

I carried her sturdy little form into the living room, giving her a kiss or two before I set her down in front of our puzzle. She didn't need my help, but she liked it when I watched. After she was asleep and I was in my pajamas, reading in bed, Airik came into our bedroom.

"Is Lalla asleep?" he asked, giving me a kiss.

I nodded.

He pulled his T-shirt off, giving me a view of his well-muscled chest. I lifted my eyebrows at him. He gave me a sexy smile that I loved. Then he took off his pants and crawled into the bed wearing only his boxers.

I tingled when I saw the look in his eye.

"Do you remember what it was like before our mission, Quinn? Before I knew I loved you?"

"Yes," I said, dropping my eyes at the memories of the sadness.

"You know what?"

"What?" I asked, playing along.

"I don't. I feel like there's never been a time when I didn't love you. I can't imagine being with anyone else. I'm glad you're the mother of my daughter and future children."

I smiled and put my hand on his cheek. "Future children? That sounds optimistic. Isn't the birth rate on Koccoran something like 1.4 children per couple?"

"I don't know how people manage to have a half a kid, but I'm glad we have one whole little munchkin."

"She's enough of a handful as she is, never mind an extra 0.4. I can't imagine having as many kids as your parents. How did they manage that on this planet?"

"They're an anomaly."

"Maybe it's in the genes," I said, raising my eyebrows.

"It's definitely in the genes. I think a brother or sister for Lalla wouldn't be a bad thing."

"Of course not," I said. "It's just improbable."

"Lalla herself was improbable. I don't believe in limiting ourselves."

"What are you suggesting, Airik?"

"We should get started on a sibling for our little darling."

"I want at least two years between them." His eyes lit up at my acquiescence.

"We should start practicing." He took the computer from my hands and set it on the bedside table.

"I love you," he whispered into my ear. His English made me smile and shiver simultaneously. He trailed his fingers down my shoulder until he came to the thin spaghetti strap of my blue silk tank top. He drew it down slowly. Baring my shoulder, he kissed it, then did the same on the other side.

I slid down until I lay on my back. He sucked on my nipple through the fabric, driving me crazy. The sensations of his mouth through the silky material aroused me, and I moaned.

"Babe, you are smoking hot," he said, pulling the shirt off me to reveal my breasts. His hands covered them and massaged them, making me writhe under his touch.

"Airik," I whispered.

He knew what I needed, and his hands slid into my shorts, pulling them off along with the panties I wore underneath. He disposed of his boxers as well, lying beside me and sliding his hand down my inner thigh. As his hand brushed my sex, I gasped. He reached to cup me, letting one finger slowly open my folds.

I was already wet for him, and he rubbed me, focusing on my hard nub.

"Please," I said desperately.

He rolled onto his back. He knew I liked to straddle him. There were no artificial barriers between us, of course, since it was against the law to have protected sex on Koccoran. All babies were desired, even if the parents didn't want to raise them.

I lifted myself and carefully positioned my opening, letting myself down an inch at a time onto him until we joined. My breath was coming in short bursts. He reached up and twisted my nipples, making me even more aroused.

"I love how you look when you're sitting on me, Quinn. You're a sex goddess," he said, his eyes cloudy with lust.

I didn't answer him. I lifted myself up and took him deep inside me again. Oh, fuck that felt good. I rode him slowly until I couldn't stand it anymore.

"Now?" he asked, and I nodded. I was so close to orgasm that I couldn't speak. He rolled us over, being careful to keep us coupled together. He pinned me under his hard, hot body and began driving into me quickly, the way I liked it at the end.

The pleasure built until I couldn't stand it any longer. When he dipped his head to take one of my breasts into his mouth, I cried out and came. He put his hand over my mouth to stifle any more sounds. He was always paranoid we would wake Lalla. I pressed my lips together as spasms overtook my body. My hips moved against him as he continued to pound into me, looking for his release.

After another minute, I felt him stiffen and fill me with his seed. His orgasm sent me off into another round of aftershocks until finally I lay still in a state of bliss. He kissed my chest, lifting his dead weight off of me. Then he gave one of my nipples a suck, making me spasm again. I moaned, and he smiled, lying down and pressing his body against mine.

"I love you," I whispered to him in English.

"I love you, too," he said in his language.

A vision rocked the both of us, showing our fiftieth anniversary, surrounded by children and grandchildren. We saw ourselves kissing like we were still young.

I looked at him for confirmation that he had seen it as well.

"I counted five, at least," he said, kissing my forehead.

"At least five what?"

"Kids," he said proudly.

"Well," I said. "I'll give you an hour's rest, but then we'll have to practice some more. Five children will be hard work."

"An hour," he snorted. "I'm not an old man yet."

"Oh, really?" I said, grinning. "Why don't you show me?"

And he did.

If you enjoyed this book, please review it on Amazon. Your review helps me succeed as an author.

To stay up-to-date on my latest releases, sign up for my newsletter at:

http://lisalace.com/newsletter/

OTHER BOOKS BY LISA LACE

WATER WORLD WARRIOR: A TERRAMATES NOVEL

Why would I want to be married to an alien?

I should not have applied to TerraMates! The idea was crazy. I'm a young woman, in the prime of my life.

But I was desperate.

When I landed on another world, his appearance intrigued me. He dripped sexuality and moved like an animal. We have three days together before he sets sail without me. Am I going to escape or submit to my desires?

TAKEN: A TERRAMATES NOVEL

What happens when TerraMates runs out of applicants?

There's never a shortage of wealthy alien bachelors looking for the thrill of mating with a human. They want our women.

But despite the promise of riches, sometimes the pool of available brides runs dry.

How does TerraMates find more girls, and where do they go? When Lyzette gets taken off the street, she finds out.

Water World Confidential: A TerraMates Novel

He needed a wife. I wanted an alien lover.

The first time I saw Jori, I hated everything about him. He didn't care about anything except himself. On the other hand, his body was spectacular, and his muscles were firm. I couldn't stop thinking about him.

When TerraMates gave me the chance to marry Jori, I took it. I knew I needed the money. What I didn't know was that Jori's exterior was a facade, and he had kept secrets from everyone his entire life.

Captured by the Alien King

When I saw my chance to get off Earth, I took it. I knew I needed to escape.

I didn't know I'd be claimed by an alien monarch in the middle of his mating season! Now we're on the run together, facing terrorists and natural disasters.

I'm still trying to figure out my feelings for this sexy guy. He is totally into me, but he has some unique ideas about alien romance…